ROMANCE

W9-BXL-702

WITHDRAWN

STACKS

DEC 10 1997

A BUSINESS
ENGAGEMENT

A BUSINESS ENGAGEMENT

BY

JESSICA STEELE

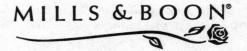

MILLS & BOON®

*MILLS & BOON and
MILLS & BOON with the Rose Device
are registered trademarks of the publisher.*

*First published in Great Britain 1997
Large Print edition 1997
Harlequin Mills & Boon Limited,
Eton House, 18-24 Paradise Road,
Richmond, Surrey TW9 1SR*

© *Jessica Steele 1997*

ISBN 0 263 15171 9

*Set in Times Roman
16-9708-60720 C15½-16½*

*Printed and bound in Great Britain
by Mackays of Chatham PLC, Chatham*

CHAPTER ONE

ASHLYN stirred, remembered what day it was and was instantly wide awake. She wanted with all she had to go back to sleep again.

Though, bearing in mind that she had been dreading today ever since she had first known about it, it was a wonder to her that she had slept at all!

It had been a complete and utter bombshell, the *whole* of it, when some weeks ago now, her father had announced that he had sold his company, Ainsworth Cables. She'd realised that there had been one or two signs along the way, but that had been *afterwards*.

Prior to her father's disclosure, her friend Todd Pilkington had questioned, 'I say, Ash, any truth in the rumour I heard today that Ainsworth Cables is up for grabs?' She had denied this at once, and it had been too laughable for her even to remember to mention it to her father. Not that she saw too much of him: he worked hard, and if he wasn't working he and her mother would be out socialising

5

somewhere. And, Ashlyn admitted, she had a lot of friends, male and female, of her own, and was frequently out herself.

On that particular night, her father had been late in and had joined them in the dining room after she and her mother had sat down to dinner. Ashlyn was halfway through her meal and, having a flair for languages, was silently mulling over the possibility of taking a stab at Japanese, when she all at once had become aware of a certain tension in the air.

She'd looked to her mother—a young fifty, beautiful, intelligent and with a mind of her own—and a reputation for being one of the most charming hostesses around. Her mother had caught her looking at her, had given a half-smile, and turned her attention to her husband.

Neville Ainsworth was sixty, had thinning hair and wore glasses and was known to be a shrewd businessman. Which was why it had been such a total shock when, as Ashlyn had sensed telepathic messages going between her parents, he had all at once announced, 'Well, it's sold.'

Ashlyn hadn't known he had been selling anything, and had wondered briefly if he was thinking of exchanging his car. But, somehow, she'd sensed from the tension in the air that there was something rather more involved than any mere motor vehicle.

'Signed?' her mother queried. Ashlyn looked from her father back to her mother—clearly she knew what it was that had been sold.

'And sealed—and paid for,' Neville Ainsworth replied, and her mother smiled. What was going on?

'And Ashlyn? They agreed...?'

Ashlyn stared at her mother and gave up all pretence of being interested in her meal. 'Me?' she butted in. 'What's sold? What's signed and sealed? And,' she added, as yet nothing too dramatic happening to disturb the calm waters of her life, 'where do I come into it?'

She transferred her gaze to her father, her large green eyes resting sensitively on him. She had known all her life that it was a bitter disappointment to him that she was not the son he'd wanted—and that her mother, after a difficult birth, had firmly declined to risk the experience a second time.

She saw her father look to his wife, and was totally astonished when he calmly revealed, 'I've sold Ainsworth Cables.'

'You've sold...?' She couldn't take it in. 'But...but...' Good grief! The intelligence she had inherited from both her parents began to function—you didn't just wake up one morning and decide to sell a company as large as her father's and—hey presto!—by dinnertime the deal was done! 'How? Why?' she asked incredulously, in truth feeling just a tiny bit put out that this was the first she had heard of it. 'How long has it been on the market?'

'Not too long,' her mother came in, using some of her ample charm. 'Naturally we'd have told you sooner—when—er—negotiations began—but we didn't want word to get out.'

Ashlyn recalled Todd Pilkington's question of ages ago as to whether there was any truth in the rumour that the firm was for sale. Word *had* got out, but, just now, that was beside the point—how had her father thought he could keep a thing like this quiet? He had, though, to a large extent, hadn't he? For apart from that one hint from Todd this was the first she'd heard of it.

'But why?' she just had to ask then. 'Why sell? You love work. *Love* the work you do. Love the—'

'I didn't have much choice,' her father cut in bluntly. 'And if you let that go further than these four walls I'll...'

He didn't finish. He didn't have to. All her life she had been aware of his mammoth pride, a pride her mother had in abundance too—it was something else which Ashlyn had inherited.

'You're saying that the firm is—was,' she hastily corrected, Ainsworth Cables no longer being theirs, 'in some sort of difficulty?'

'You could say that,' her father answered offhandedly. Clearly he did not want to talk about it.

But Ashlyn was already feeling shut out, excluded, and didn't like it. They were a family, for goodness' sake, and if something was going wrong then she wanted to be included, involved.

'Financial?' she questioned. Despite the fact that money had always *seemed* to be readily available, this could be the only answer.

'Financial,' he agreed heavily.

'Oh, Daddy, why didn't you say? I could have sold my car, got a job. I could—'

'And let everyone know we were up against it?' her mother cut her off acidly, her charm gone. 'No, thank you very much. We're worth a little more than that!' Pride, Ashlyn realised, was the reason why her parents had wanted everything kept secret. 'Not that selling your car and getting some dreary little job would have saved the company,' Katherine Ainsworth added. 'Unfortunately, your father made

some—ahem—' she coughed, as though it
might soften what she had to say '—some
rather ill-advised decisions which—I'm sorry,
Neville...' She looked at him and continued,
'Which cost the company dear—and from
which we were unable to recover. Ainsworth
Cables had been losing money ever since—in
fact, had been going steadily downhill.'

'I see,' Ashlyn murmured, aware that her
father must be feeling dreadful. Or was he?
Surely by now, with the company sold and
her father affluent again—albeit without a
company to run—he would not be feeling so
dreadful as when he'd had to make the decision
to sell? 'But if the firm's been going downhill
who on earth did you find to buy it?' She
owned she had the least businesslike brain of
anyone she knew, but even she just couldn't see
any company buying another company which,
by the sound of it, was on its last legs.

'Your father might be down, but he's certainly not out!' her mother rebuked her stiffly.
And, with a smile to her husband, she continued, 'In fact he's managed to pull off a deal
that is not only advantageous to the new owners
and to ourselves, but which has enabled us to
come out of this with our pride intact.'

'Well, I always knew he was pretty clever.' Ashlyn smiled, only too glad that, by the sound of it, her father had not after all come out of this too badly dented. 'So—who did you sell Ainsworth Cables to?'

Husband and wife exchanged what could only be called smug glances. 'Hamilton Holdings.' Ashlyn's father beat her mother to it.

'Hamilton Holdings!' Ashlyn exclaimed. Good heavens, they were a massive group of companies! And, while Ainsworth Cables was no pint-sized outfit either, from what her father had just been saying she could not see one good reason why such a prosperous conglomerate would have wanted to take on an ailing firm. 'I know you had a wonderful company...' she attempted to soften the question '...but why, if things were as bad as you say, would a group like Hamilton's have wanted to take us over?'

'Because they're a forward-planning company, that's why.' Ashlyn was lost. She guessed it showed, because her father went on, looking smug again, 'I happened to know that they own the land on either side of my factory and offices.'

'Ah!' A fragile light started to break through.

'Forward planning for any company means thinking not of today, but of five, ten, twenty years from now,' her father continued. 'Hamilton Holdings couldn't have given a tuppenny damn about what my company produced, or how successful it was. The land it stood on, now, that was a very different matter.'

'Your—possession of it—could have held up their future plans?' Ashlyn guessed.

'And how! It's a prime site! I'd known for years that they'd be first in with an offer should I ever consider selling. Carter Hamilton himself came to see me. But when I'd stated my price—and Hamilton Holdings weren't the only people interested, believe me—we got bogged down on—er—one very important issue.'

The name Carter Hamilton meant little to her, though she guessed he must be some very big noise in the Hamilton tree. Just as she guessed what that one very important issue was. 'Your employees' welfare?' she suggested.

She realised she was wrong when her father shook his head. 'Oh, their jobs are secure enough for the time being,' he stated. But then he went on, 'We're talking *forward planning* here. Hamilton's are in no great rush, except that the Ainsworth Cables site is the centre, the linchpin if you like, of what they must have, and what their competitors want—land.'

My word, all this had gone on and she'd never known! 'So you eventually managed to settle the one very important issue that was bogging the deal down.' Ashlyn was feeling quite remorseful that, unbeknown to her, her father—and her mother too to some degree— had had a very worrying time of it just lately.

'It took some doing,' Neville Ainsworth admitted, 'but, yes, they at last agreed on that very important issue. And we, as a family, are once more solvent. Mmm—extremely solvent.' He smiled, her mother smiled, and because they both looked so happy Ashlyn began to smile too. In fact her lovely smile was well in evidence when her father, with a meaningful kind of glance to her mother—which Ashlyn didn't have time to try to decipher—added, 'All that remains is for me to tell you about that very important issue.' His smile was suddenly gone, and she had rarely seen him more resolute than when he stated, 'Because it concerns you.'

Ashlyn was vaguely aware that at the outset of this conversation her mother had implied that it had something to do with her and some agreement. She began to feel a mite apprehensive. Her mother had some warm and wonderful traits, but it was not unknown for her to take a very tough line if she had to.

Ashlyn was aware of two pairs of eyes fixed on her, and her feeling of apprehension grew. Even while she had not the slightest idea of how she could figure in any sell-out of her father's business, she was all at once extremely wary.

'Me?' she questioned for the second time. 'What . . .?'

'You're a very lucky girl, Ashlyn,' her father beamed. 'Not many young women—' He broke off, and Ashlyn intercepted a look from her mother which clearly said 'Get on with it'. Her father at once changed tack. 'They've told me they're going to continue to use the name Ainsworth Cables for the foreseeable future. Not unnaturally, since I've sweated and toiled all hours for that firm, it was important to me that an Ainsworth still had something to do with it.'

'You're going to keep on working there—in some sort of management capacity?' Ashlyn guessed.

'Like hell!' her father snorted—and she saw she had just accidentally rubbed salt into the raw wound of his pride. But before she could rush in to offer an apology he promptly and baldly announced, 'The company manager's job was offered in exchange for what I wanted. But I stuck it out. The result, my dear, is that I've managed to negotiate a seat on the board of Hamilton Holdings—for you.'

Ashlyn's brain went numb. She played back in her head what her father had just said. It still didn't sound any better. 'You're joking?' she hoped.

'I was never more serious. I sold out for a substantial amount of cash, a tidy few shares—and a seat on the board for you.'

'But—but...' Words failed her. 'The board of Hamilton Holdings?' Perhaps she'd heard him incorrectly.

'It wasn't easy.'

She bet it wasn't. She bet this Carter Hamilton had offered her father everything else under the sun before he'd agreed to what her father was sticking out for. A prime site! It must be!

'But I don't know the first thing about being a board member!' she protested, and still she didn't believe it. She—a board member of Hamilton Holdings! Ye gods!

'You don't have to know anything,' her mother came in calmly, and, realising she had panicked unnecessarily, Ashlyn started to relax a little.

'Oh, you mean it's just one of those nominal things: my name is on the paper, but I don't actually have to do anything.'

'Of course you have to do something!' Abruptly her mother's tone had changed.

Oh, heavens, her mother was getting on her high horse! Even so, Ashlyn felt she just could not accept what had been arranged for her without question, without some sort of protest. 'But why me? Why not Father?'

'Because your father has always been his own boss, that's why,' her mother stated angrily. 'Can you honestly see him taking orders from somebody else? His pride would never allow it.'

Pride again! But, so far as Ashlyn knew, board members didn't have to take orders from anyone—or did they? It all proved how little she did know, she realised.

She tried to say as much. 'But I don't know anything at all about the business world. About—'

'I've already told you that you don't have to!' Katherine Ainsworth reminded her sharply. 'But this way we'll be able to salvage some pride, and we'll stop your father's brothers from speculating that he *had* to sell, when they hear how badly Hamilton Holdings want you on their board.'

Uncle Edward and Uncle Richard wouldn't be fooled for a minute! They knew as much as anybody that she wouldn't know a balance sheet if she tripped over one. And did they pass balance sheets around at board meetings anyhow?

This was ridiculous. Totally ridiculous. 'But—why me?' she asked. If not her father, then surely her mother would be better able to sit on the board than—

'Why not you?' her mother cut through her thoughts. 'Your father has worked hard all these years to support you and see that you've wanted for nothing!' Ashlyn was staring, stupefied and shaken by such an attack, as her mother ended, 'It won't hurt you to do something for him for a change.'

Ashlyn normally had a very good relationship with her mother, given that her mother could occasionally be a bit sharp. But she was fairly staggered to have her round on her in this way, especially since her mother knew full well that she had been keen to train for a career—a career where she would have been able to support herself. Only her mother had objected. Ashlyn did not feel that now was the time to remind her of that fact. Though it was true that, apart from helping her parents entertain various business people from time to time, and act as hostess when her mother was unable, she had done little more to help her father. Not that she had been able to think of anything he wanted help with. Ah... How about he needed help—like now?

Yet, even while she was being made to feel guilty, and her protests seemed to be growing frighteningly fainter, she just had to try one more time. 'You know I've absolutely no knowledge of business, and know nothing about boardroom procedure...'

'You won't need to know anything,' her father came in bracingly. 'All you have to do is make sure you attend every board meeting. I don't want them to have the smallest excuse to part with you.'

Great! By the sound of it, the board would soon be looking for an excuse to get rid of her. Nice to feel welcome! 'But what role would I play?' Board members voted on various things, didn't they? 'Supposing I'm asked to vote on something or other. How can I vote when I don't know...?'

'You're just being difficult!' her mother sniffed. 'Stop thinking about yourself, and think of me and your father for a change!'

That hurt. It made her feel ungrateful—when she wasn't. Ashlyn was still smarting from her mother's remark when her father, as if trying to explain, began, 'I'm sure Carter Hamilton only agreed to my stipulation about you because he felt he wouldn't have to look far for a reason to get you out. But, since you'll be a non-executive member of the board, all you have to do is turn up at the monthly meeting—or whatever the frequency is—and look intelligent. That's all there'll be to it.' Her father smiled at her encouragingly. 'They can hardly remove you from the board if you don't do anything, can they?'

He made it sound simple, but Ashlyn was sure that it wasn't. But, in view of her mother's 'think of me and your father for a change', she felt bereft of more argument.

That did not stop her from fretting about it in the week that followed, though. And with each passing day she knew more and more that she most definitely did not want this job which her father had manufactured for her—be it only for a few hours a month.

How could she want it when they didn't want her? She also guessed that feeling doubled for this bod Carter Hamilton. And that was another strange thing; she'd never heard his name before, so far as she could remember, yet now his picture just seemed to jump out at her from every newspaper she picked up.

He was young, she thought, to hold such a lofty position, even if the group did bear his name—and he was good-looking with it. He appeared to be about thirty-five or thirty-six and tall—unless the elegant woman by his side in that particular picture was very tiny. Though the woman wasn't his wife, because the article, a kind of *Who's Who* at some première or other, referred to Carter Hamilton as 'chairman—and most eligible bachelor—of Hamilton Holdings'.

Ashlyn felt all churned up inside as she looked at the newspaper photograph. She was on the same board as *him*! Oh, grief. She had always felt comfortable in any company— whether hostessing for her mother when she was indisposed, or with her friends. Ashlyn had many friends, from all walks of life, and, having grown up with half a dozen male cousins—who, to a large extent, protected her and treated her more as a little sister—she was

quite comfortable in male company too. So
what was it about this man, a man whom she
hadn't even met, but whose picture she only
had to look at to feel churned up inside—and
all goosebumpy?

Rubbish, she told herself—but she felt all
churned up inside again when the next week
brought forth a letter on Hamilton Holdings
paper informing her of a board meeting two
weeks hence. She wanted to hide. With the
letter came a copy of the agenda for the
meeting. It looked complex. She read it through
twice—she knew Greek better!

A little light came into her darkness when
her youngest cousin, Duncan, telephoned to say
he was home from university that weekend, and
did she want to take him out for a drink?

'I'll do better than that—I'll take you out
and feed you, if you like.'

'When I'm a millionaire and not scratching
along on a student grant, I'll take *you* out for
a meal,' he accepted, and she laughed. His
family were loaded, and she doubted very much
he would qualify for a grant even if he applied.
But he was always broke.

Ashlyn sighed as she recalled how she had
wanted to go to university. She was keen on

languages, and had wanted to be a teacher, or perhaps take work in the translation field.

Her mother had not liked the idea, she knew. But at that time her mother had been going through a period of being unwell. Her illness had been nothing specific—just a general debility. Exhaustion, her doctor had diagnosed. Nothing that dropping a few committees and rest and care would not cure.

But Ashlyn had been seriously worried, especially when she'd heard her mother, whose energy had always been boundless, declare one afternoon that she thought she would take a nap. And, a few evenings later, she'd asked Ashlyn if she would mind standing in for her at some dinner. Ashlyn had been too concerned about her parent to give more than a passing thought to the fact she had left it too late to apply for a university place that year.

It had taken over eighteen months for her mother to fully recover, and by then Ashlyn had left school. But while her mother had begun to take an interest in shopping again Ashlyn had begun to think in terms of the subject of which she had an instinctive grasp.

She was already fluent in French and Italian—there were so many languages out there. So many challenges. 'Mother...' she'd begun one evening.

'Oh, dear. I always know it's serious when you call me Mother,' Katherine Ainsworth had teased. And as if she suspected what was coming, to Ashlyn's surprise, she'd continued, 'Actually, I meant to have a serious talk with you—only the moment never seemed right.'

'It didn't?' Ashlyn's mother was busy from dawn to dusk again, it was true, but surely...

Her mother had shaken her head. 'I've never said to you how grateful I was to have you around to hold my hand when I was so low a while back.'

'You don't have to!' Ashlyn had protested.

'Oh, but I do. I know there were times when you could have gone out with your friends but, out of concern for me, just in case I needed you, you stayed home. I have appreciated so very much your staying home when you could have gone to university.'

'I wanted to stay home.' No way, with her mother so poorly, would she have gone anywhere!

'I know. But now it's my turn to do something for you.'

'Oh, that's not necess—'

'So I've arranged for you to continue your language studies privately.'

Ashlyn could not believe it, and had felt closer to her mother then than she had at any time. Katherine Ainsworth had gone on to outline how on Mondays, Wednesdays and Fridays Ashlyn was to have language tuition.

Four years later, at twenty-two, she was fluent in several more languages, and was taking a break from studying—which left her without one single solitary excuse for being unable to attend even just one of the board meetings held at Hamilton Holdings' main office.

And the closer it got to what was looming large in her mind as Terrifying Tuesday, the more she did not want to attend.

Oh, if only... If only she'd been born the boy her father had wanted. It had been a big disappointment to him that while his brothers had sons he had a daughter. Neither he nor her mother had wanted her to go into the business and, Ashlyn had to own, she'd been quite happy about that.

Her father, the youngest of three sons, had not wanted to go into his father's business either. Consequently, with her grandfather's help, he had started up his own company.

Ainsworth Engineering, the company founded by her grandfather, was now run by her uncles and her cousins—and very prosperous it was too. With the exception of Duncan, her cousins were married and scattered round about, so that she saw much less of them these days.

It did not stop her hearing about them, though. Only last night, after her mother had asked her what she planned to wear to the board meeting today, she had remarked how her two brothers-in-law were always saying how well their sons were doing.

'Well, they are,' Ashlyn had pointed out fairly.

Her mother had not wanted to know. 'So I told Edward when he rang to speak with your father yesterday—casually, of course—how you'd be a great asset to the Hamilton Holdings board at their meeting on Tuesday!'

Now, realising she could delay starting the day no longer, Ashlyn got out of bed, with her mother's words ringing in her ears. Asset! If Uncle Edward believed that, he'd believe anything.

Pride, of course. Her mother wasn't normally boastful, but pride was dictating events these days.

Ashlyn was in the shower when she realised that she too was being dictated to by pride. Why else was she doing what she was doing? Oh, not for herself. But pride demanded that since her father had stuck out for her seat on the board as part of the deal she would have to go—he would look exceedingly silly if she didn't turn up.

How did board members dress? Well, not with a thick mane of red hair hanging all the way down their backs, that was for sure. She didn't want breakfast, indeed felt in such a turmoil inside that all she could do was hope the next three or four hours would pass quickly so that she could hurry back home.

'Darling, you look lovely!' her mother exclaimed when, her red hair pulled back and classically knotted away from her face—which that morning was almost translucent—Ashlyn presented herself downstairs. Her mother was seldom up this early.

'Is that suit new?' her father asked gruffly, so she knew that he thought she looked all right as well.

'It cost me the last of my allowance—hint, hint,' she managed to joke, and, with her parents' love and good wishes ringing in her ears, she went to get her car out of its garage.

She found the Hamilton Holdings building without too much trouble. But she was feeling so agitated that, but for remembering her mother's 'Your father has worked hard...to support you... It won't hurt you to do something for him for a change', she might have steered her car anywhere but down to Hamilton Holdings' underground car park. It didn't make her feel any better, however, to also remember—and she wished that she hadn't—that Hamilton Holdings didn't want her, and that Carter Hamilton in particular would be looking for a way to get rid of her.

There were few car parking spaces left but, since she espied security cameras, she was confident that were she to erroneously park in the chairman's allotted space, then for sure someone would hare down to turf her out.

Ashlyn rode up in the lift to the reception area and, not for the first time, wondered what the dickens she was so afraid of. Plenty, came the answer as she visualised the whole of the meeting taking place with never so much as a peep coming from her. She knew nothing!

She was glad of her new suit, though; it was light navy—a businesslike touch, she felt. She also wore a pristine white fine jersey collarless shirt, which crossed over her bosom in a few softly rolled pleats.

She went up to the reception desk on plain navy two-and-a-half inch heels. 'My name's Ashlyn Ainsworth—can you direct me to the boardroom, please?' she asked.

She was expected. Pity. 'Certainly, Miss Ainsworth,' the receptionist smiled, and in no time a uniformed attendant was there to escort her up, not to the actual boardroom, but to a kind of ante-room.

It was ten to ten. The meeting would start on the hour. The next five minutes passed in something of a blank, stomach-swirling haze. 'How do you do?' She shook a lot of hands. 'How do you do?' At least she was dressed properly for it.

Dark-suited, white-haired, brown-haired, no-haired men came within her orbit. But as yet there was no one looking remotely like the dark-haired man she'd seen in the newspapers.

There was then a general move towards the boardroom, and a friendly voice stated, 'You're a decided improvement on this lot.' Manna from heaven! 'I'm Geoffrey Rogers, by the way. And you just have to be Ashlyn Ainsworth.'

She shook hands with him and Geoffrey, a man of about forty, escorted her into the boardroom, kindly showing her where to sit. Then he went to take his own seat about four chairs along, and during the next couple of minutes Ashlyn got a sketchy impression, from a word drifting down from here and there, that board members had flown in from all corners to be there today.

She glanced shyly about, and realised with a sinking feeling that she was the only female present. Oh, grief, had she invaded an all-male board?

But then another female did come in, complete with notebook and pencils. If she's waiting to record anything I might say, Ashlyn thought, she'd have a long wait. Then a kind of hush seemed to descend over the boardroom—and *he* was there.

He *was* tall, as she had thought. Ashlyn was tallish herself, but guessed he was six or seven inches taller. Still he hadn't noticed her sitting there—the man next to her was rather large. Perhaps it would stay that way.

He was every bit as good-looking as he'd appeared in the newspapers, though. And self-assured with it, she realised. 'Good morning,' he greeted everyone generally; he was clearly a man with little time to waste. 'We've a lot to get through,' he continued, his voice cultured

and all male, 'but before we start I should like
to open this meeting by first introducing, and
welcoming, our newest member, Miss Ashlyn
Ainsworth.'

Oh, my giddy aunt! And she'd thought he
hadn't even noticed her! Ashlyn found herself
pinned by a pair of stern dark eyes. And, as
she quickly realised that there was little that this
man missed, all other eyes turned to her. She
wanted the floor to open up and swallow her—
oh, how she wished that the next few hours
were over!

CHAPTER TWO

QUITE when Ashlyn had begun to dislike Carter Hamilton she couldn't have said. Probably before she had ever met him—and it was nothing to do with the fact that his organisation had bought out her father's firm. Somebody or other would have done that anyway since, as Todd Pilkington had so eloquently put it, the company had been 'up for grabs'.

But dislike Carter Hamilton she did. Even as the meeting got under way and attention moved from her, she decided that she did not like him. Welcoming her! He'd been lying through his teeth!

She gave her attention to the meeting, but inside a very few minutes knew that she was out of her depth. Big business was life's blood to these people—she was having a hard time making sense of any of it.

She concentrated harder—and found herself watching Carter Hamilton. She tried to forget him and focus instead on the business to hand—but, since he was constantly in her line of vision, she found that that was extremely difficult.

Carter, obviously, was having no such problem. Not once had he glanced her way since that initial eye contact. Clearly she was beneath his notice.

Who the devil did he think he was? Feeling riled, Ashlyn concentrated more determinedly on forgetting his presence and tuned into what had begun quite sensibly but had soon degenerated into total gibberish as far as she was concerned. She was good at languages, but they seemed to be speaking a language she had never heard before.

Figures, in millions, were tossed around like confetti. Someone, although still seated, verbally took the floor to give a lengthy and totally boring report—and Ashlyn strove to look enrapt.

She gave an inward sigh of relief when the report ended, and she wondered what the time was. It was tempting to take a look at her watch—but she did not want to draw attention to herself. There was a clock in the boardroom—but its face was just out of her line of vision.

She did a head count—they were sixteen altogether. Seventeen including the PA taking down the minutes. Carter Hamilton had rather a nice-shaped head...

Abruptly Ashlyn switched her glance from him—and caught sight of the watch on the wrist of the large man next to her. Was it only a quarter past ten? Oh, no—it couldn't be! It wasn't—she'd read it wrong. And later, when the dull-as-ditchwater meeting seemed to have been going on for hours, it was not very heartening to realise that it was only a quarter to eleven.

Try to get interested. You're intelligent—it said so on your school report. And you have A levels to prove it. But 'feasible', 'viable', 'expedient'? Not to mention 'resource', and 'finance'. 'Equilateral' somehow got in too— which was enough to let her know her full attention had slipped some five minutes ago.

Relief was at hand when someone knocked on the boardroom door and wheeled in some coffee. 'Black or white?' enquired the pleasant young woman when she got round to Ashlyn.

'White, please,' Ashlyn smiled—and that was about as much relief as she got, for the meeting carried on through coffee.

Her father had hinted that these meetings happened once a month—once a year would be too much in her view. Perhaps if she'd been born to it, had started there as a junior, worked her way up to the position which, without any training whatsoever she had just been tossed into—perhaps then she would have comprehended—and even enjoyed—this language everyone was talking.

Yet another new language was foisted on her when a short while later some high-powered legal eagle came in to outline the wherefores of what could be done, and the therefores of why something else could not.

He went on and on, in a dull, monotone voice, and was still going on when Ashlyn glanced about her. Everyone seemed totally absorbed—she had never felt so inadequate! Everybody knew so much more than she did; even the woman taking the minutes knew more—not once did her pencil falter.

The legal executive had been talking for what seemed to be three days when Ashlyn gave up. She saw him pause to pour himself a glass of water. She reckoned he needed it. She too needed a drink, anything to waken her up— she had an idea she'd be asleep in a minute. But, as before, she did not want to draw at-

tention to herself by stretching out an arm to
the carafe of water in front of her.

Her thoughts drifted and she wondered how
long the PA had had to train for this high level
of work. The woman was about thirty...
Suddenly Ashlyn realised that her eyelids were
drooping and, terror-stricken that she might
nod off—or, worse, start snoring in the middle
of this top-brass meeting—she stretched out an
arm to the water carafe, and, in her haste,
knocked it over!

She stared, disbelieving, as the water emptied
from the half-pint carafe. She came to life only
as the cascade headed for the important-
looking papers and notes belonging to the men
seated on either side of her—and did the only
thing possible. She grabbed hold of the pad in
front of her—with not a single scribbled note
on it—and hastily directed the water her own
way.

She had, she discovered, found one very
good way of getting the legal person to shut up.
Indeed, as water soaked her lap, all that could
be heard was a deathly silence.

She wanted to die. She knew her pale skin
was scarlet as she looked up from her sodden
skirt—and met the hard-eyed glance of the
chairman full-on. His expression was grim. Oh,

Lord! And she hadn't wanted to draw attention to herself!

Mortified, she cringed inwardly. But it was perhaps out of mortification that pride came to her aid. As she saw it, she had two choices: either she sat there dripping water onto the carpet—a humiliation she did not need—or she got out of there.

She got to her feet and, refusing to whisper—she who had not intended to say a word at this meeting—tilted her chin a proud fraction. Addressing the whole of the board, she stated, 'It seems I need to go and get dried out!' Oh, brilliant—she sounded like some half-demented alcoholic!

Ashlyn went quickly, her face burning. She headed for the door, but someone got there before her. She looked up, and her humiliation was complete. Without saying a word Carter Hamilton opened the door.

She did not thank him, although he had left his place at the board table to come and open the door for her. With her head still in the air she sailed out from the meeting—and heard the door close behind her with a decisive click.

The pig! The swine! If that wasn't saying 'And don't come back' she didn't know what was! Not that she would dream of going back—ever.

Having passed through the ante-room, she somehow—though how, when the many-storeyed building was a maze of corridors and offices, she wasn't sure—managed to find the ladies' room. She looked down at her skirt and very nearly gave way to tears.

She hadn't wanted to come, wished she hadn't, and no doubt the whole of the boardroom had erupted into laughter the moment that door had shut. Oh, confound it!

Ashlyn was in the middle of reiterating to herself that the whole idea of her being a member of the board was ridiculous anyway, when the ladies'-room door opened. She looked up as an overall-clad, motherly-looking woman of about fifty came bustling in.

The woman took just one look at Ashlyn's skirt and, with a cheerful calm that said she took everything in her stride, said, 'You're Miss Ainsworth, and I'm Ivy, the general indispensable dogsbody around here.'

'You know me?' Ashlyn queried, blaming the slowness of her brain on the fact that she had worried so much last night that she had barely slept. Perhaps that had contributed to her almost falling asleep in that ghastly meeting.

'Just your name. Word came down from the boardroom that I should get into my Wonderwoman outfit and find you. You can't go out like that!' Ivy rattled on. 'If you'll come with me, I'll have you sorted in no time.'

By then Ashlyn was happy to have someone else attempt miracles. Though where she was going she had no idea as, chatting nineteen to the dozen, Ivy took her on a journey via corridors and a lift. Who was it who'd instructed Ivy to find her? Certainly not *him*!

'This is my cubby-hole,' Ivy announced brightly, showing Ashlyn into a room that was an Aladdin's cave of brushes, brooms and buckets, with a chair, a table, a box of new tights and an ironing board. Ah! 'If you'll let me have your skirt...'

'I can do it,' Ashlyn smiled, getting out of her skirt and already starting to feel more human.

'Of course you can,' Ivy agreed cheerfully, and made Ashlyn laugh when she added, 'But it's my iron and my ironing board.'

Ashlyn handed her skirt over and, having had so many words bounced around her in the boardroom, found it a balm to be able to talk and have a normal conversation for a change as she watched Ivy go to work.

In no time—or perhaps time was passing quicker now that she was away from the boardroom—her skirt was blotted with a clean towel, dried with a hairdryer, and finally pressed.

'Fancy a cup of tea while we're waiting for your skirt to settle?' Ivy asked.

'I'd love one,' Ashlyn agreed, and was beamed at by Ivy, who, to Ashlyn's mind, was more the wonderwoman than the dogsbody she had first described herself as.

By the time she was dressed again and had finished her tea, Ashlyn felt much better. And, her equilibrium restored, she sincerely thanked Ivy for her help.

'You look better than you did,' Ivy remarked. And, as Ashlyn went to leave, she added, 'I'm going your way; I'll come with you.'

Ashlyn had no idea where in the vast building they were, and was grateful again to Ivy when she led her once more through a maze of corridors and to the lift.

Courtesy to the older woman made her hold back when Ivy pressed the button for the top floor. That was where the boardroom was, but even if her life had depended upon it, Ashlyn knew she could not go back in there. The

boring meeting was probably still going on—
she'd die rather than cause a commotion by
going back to take her place.

Her intention to wait until Ivy left the lift
and to then press the button marked 'Parking'
was not fulfilled. For even as the doors opened
and she smiled, 'Thank you again, Ivy,' indicating that she was going to another floor as
Ivy got out, a mature male she recognised as
having been at the board meeting came around
the corner. He spotted the lift was open and
made for it.

Ashlyn had no option but to put a finger on
the button to hold the doors open. She had to
keep it there for some while, for as he got in
someone else came around the corner—and
someone else. Oh, no! Not *him*!

Carter Hamilton nodded, but otherwise ignored her. She was aware of him, though.
Aware that he had moved to stand just behind
her. So aware of him was she that she could
almost imagine his breath on the back of her
neck.

Someone else got in. She took a step back—
and came up against a firm body. Her breath
caught. She felt suddenly electrified. Hastily
she took a step to the right—and realised that
he must have felt too close for comfort too, for

he moved a fraction to the left. She looked down, caught sight of one very expensively clad foot. She quickly looked up again and, just as someone else pressed the ground-floor button and the lift doors started to close, Geoffrey Rogers—friendly Geoffrey Rogers—hared in.

'Ah, Ashlyn!' he exclaimed, ignoring the others and sounding pleased to see her. 'All mended?'

He made her deluging of the boardroom table, and consequently herself, sound an everyday occurrence. She warmed to him. 'Ivy's a marvel,' she smiled, wanting quite desperately to get out of the lift. She found Carter Hamilton totally unsettling.

'We can all testify to that. Broken shoelaces replaced, buttons...' He halted. 'You're joining us for lunch, of course?' he queried, clearly expecting her to say yes. She stared at him, wondering if it was the done thing after a board meeting for everyone to go and have a meal somewhere.

She was about to refuse; another helping of boardroom talk, even if helped down by a first-class meal, was something she had no appetite for. Then, all at once, she became aware of a tense kind of stiffness emanating from the man with the expensively clad feet.

'You're all going?' she queried pleasantly, saving herself to tell him that even if it meant she never ate again she was ducking out of this one.

'Only a few of us. We're entertaining a couple of overseas visitors.' Geoffrey Rogers smiled a warm, inviting and encouraging smile. 'Do come,' he urged, and kindly made it sound as if he would be devastated if she did not.

Quite why, instead of declining straight away, she flicked her glance upwards over her shoulder to the man on her left she could not have said. He was so close—but oh, so distant! So close that she could read nothing but hostility in his eyes. So distant that she was positive he was one of the few who would be entertaining their overseas visitors, and certain he did not want her there.

Feeling a touch shaken, she faced the front again. So, OK, he was the big cheese around here, but what right did that give him to look down his nose at anyone?

Ashlyn opened her mouth to turn down Geoffrey's invitation, and only realised how much Carter Hamilton's arrogant attitude had roused her pride when she heard herself brightly accepting, 'It sounds like fun!'

Geoffrey Rogers' face was lit by a huge grin of pleasure, then the lift halted and they all piled out into a couple of waiting chauffeur-driven limousines.

Ashlyn was thankful that she was in the vehicle that contained Geoffrey and another man—Carter Hamilton was in the one ahead. Oh, how she disliked him. So what the heck was she doing voluntarily having lunch with him?

She could find no answer to that, but decided, since she was sure she now felt hungry, that to have lunch was not such a bad idea. And anyhow, since there were to be overseas visitors present, it was a certainty that boring boardroom business would not be a subject for discussion.

The vehicle she was travelling in was caught in a sudden traffic snarl-up. Trust Carter Hamilton's car to go sailing through! So by the time they arrived at the eating establishment he was already there—as were their guests—and engaged in affable discussion.

Carter gave her a curt look as she approached but she ignored him and went into hostess mode. And he, to reluctantly give credit where it was due, put aside whatever he was feeling, and sounded almost pleasant as he in-

troduced her to the two Americans, William
Trevitt and Fitzgerald Unger. Both were warm
and friendly, approaching their late forties and
easy to get along with.

'What will you have to drink, Ashlyn?'
Carter asked.

Kind of him to ask—poison, she knew,
would have been his choice. She would be
driving later and almost asked for a mineral
water but quickly changed her mind. She didn't
want him or anyone else to recall that she had
wanted a drink of water back in the
boardroom—but had not managed to have
one.

'Orange juice, please,' she requested, as
pleasant as Carter in front of the two visitors.
Carter gave the order to a hovering waiter and
all eight of them took to chairs and couches.
'Are your family with you on this trip, Mr
Trevitt?' Ashlyn enquired of the American
seated nearest to her.

'Call me Bill,' he invited, and went on to tell
her how his wife had been unable to accompany him because of her mother's ill
health, and how, on the next trip, come what
may, he was going to insist that she come.

Ashlyn, with one notable exception, sincerely liked people, and just as sincerely was

interested in them. And so she passed a very pleasant five minutes in conversation with Bill Trevitt. She listened intently too, and automatically included others in their conversation. But she was glad that Carter and Fitzgerald Unger were seated far enough away not to need to be included.

She found herself sitting in between Fitzgerald Unger and Geoffrey Rogers at lunch, and was not sure what to make of Geoffrey when, in the manner of Bill Trevitt, he asked her not to call him Mr Rogers but to call him Geoff.

'Thank you,' she smiled. She caught Carter Hamilton's frowning glance on her and wondered what she'd done now! Clearly Geoff Rogers was a little bit of a flirt—and at his age he should know better! But that flirtatiousness had been lacking when Bill Trevitt had suggested straightforwardly that she call him Bill.

But, Geoff being a flirt aside, she had sorely needed a friend that day, and he had been the only one to welcome her with any show of friendship.

So she ignored Carter Hamilton's frowning glances and, while eating her meal, chatted either to Geoff or more particularly, since he was their guest, to Fitzgerald Unger.

She found Mr Unger an enjoyable man to talk to, and learned he had two sons at college, and a daughter born after a gap of ten years.

'I can tell you love her to pieces,' Ashlyn smiled.

'She's pretty cute—even if I do say so myself,' he agreed proudly, adding, 'And, if I may say so, you're pretty cute yourself.' Ashlyn was just about to murmur 'Thank you', for there was nothing in any way over-familiar about him, when he tacked on, 'And very, very young to be a member of Carter's board. You must be one very bright lady.'

Oh, don't tell him! She silently begged that no one who had a mind to would explain exactly how she came to be a board member. It would be just too humiliating. 'Oh, I don't know about that,' she mumbled, starting to feel a little pink as she realised that all conversation had ceased, and that everyone had heard the last part of Mr Unger's conversation. 'Actually,' she went on to confide, as she somehow felt she must, 'today's board meeting was my first.'

'Not too bad, was it?' Bill Trevitt chipped in, plainly a man who ran a board of his own, and who was aware of how awesome a first meeting might be to a junior member.

'Not too bad,' she lied with a smile.

Bill smiled and it seemed he could not resist asking her chairman, 'How did Ashlyn shape up, Carter?'

Carter looked from him to her, and under the tablecloth she crossed her fingers and prayed he would lie sooner than let a member of his board down——while at the same time acknowledging that he hadn't grown to be such a figure of trust by lying to people. Carter, to her horror, slowly drawled, 'Let's put it this way——the minutes of the meeting should make some very interesting reading.'

No! She didn't believe it! She had an idea that, by law, minutes had to be taken, but they didn't have to be a record of everything, did they? Oh, heavens——surely the PA hadn't taken down how she'd water-marked the highly polished table, and had followed that by giving herself a jolly good drenching?

'Can't wait to see them!' she heard herself chirrup; she was down but not out! 'May I ask how many members you have on your board, Bill?' She swiftly and, she hoped, not too obviously moved the conversation away from herself. 'Or, forgive me, is that something I shouldn't ask?' Having revealed just how raw a recruit she was to this game, she sat out-

wardly composed, glad that no one knew what
a mass of anguish she was feeling inside.

'Not at all. It's common knowledge,' Bill
Trevitt obliged. 'Fitz here is my deputy. But besides him . . .'

Talk centred on business procedures in their
two countries for a while. Geoff Rogers did not
take part, though. Whilst everyone else was engaged in another conversation, he asked Ashlyn
where in London she lived. 'You do live in
London?' he queried.

'Hertfordshire,' she replied.

'You came in by train?'

'By car. I left my car in Hamilton Holdings'
car park.'

'Damn—and I was going to offer to drive
you home,' he said regretfully.

Because she couldn't quite gauge if he was
serious, teasing or flirting, Ashlyn did the only
thing possible—she laughed. And at once felt
herself pinned by a pair of dark disapproving
eyes. Ye gods—now what had she done? She'd
had just about enough of *him*!

She turned her head. She was fed up with
Carter Hamilton, he of the smouldering look.
But as she chatted a moment or two more with
Geoff Rogers she was very much aware of a
pair of annoyed dark eyes watching her.

So she smiled at Geoff as if hanging on his every word—while the dislike in her heart for the chairman quietly festered. It was plain that he resented her being at this lunch—she was beginning to wish she had never come! Dratted pride.

And it was just as plain to her—even if he was masking it from the others—that Carter Hamilton was furious she was part of his board. Well, if he was so furious, he should never have done that deal with her father in the first place.

Ashlyn began to feel a bit better when she realised just how badly Carter Hamilton must have wanted her father's firm. Or, rather, the site it stood on. So huff and puff to you, she thought defiantly, and started to change her mind about not turning up for the next board meeting—she might go, just for the sheer hell of it.

'I expect you know London well,' she turned to chat comfortably with Fitzgerald Unger.

'I lived here for a year one time,' he answered, and they talked about various parts of London that they enjoyed until lunch drew to an end.

How it happened Ashlyn was never sure. But one moment they were leaving the restaurant, to mill about outside, and the next the others had gone off in the two limousines that had driven up out of nowhere and she was left standing on the pavement alone with Carter Hamilton.

He hailed a taxi—naturally one came at once. 'May I give you a lift back to your car?'

He made it sound like an order! Despite that 'May I' he was ordering her around! Well, did she have news for him!

She stared up at him, up into uncompromising, stern dark eyes. She realised that while taking part in the other conversation at the lunch table he must also have been listening to herself and Geoff Rogers—or how else could he know that she'd driven in and where she'd parked her car? She refused to be intimidated by him.

'Thanks, but no!' she answered shortly. Take a lift with him? She'd sooner crawl!

His eyes narrowed. Oh, my word! He wasn't used to anybody refusing to accept his orders, was he? That made them even. She wasn't used to being bossed about either.

She did not care for the glint that came into his eyes, though, and very definitely did not like his words when, not mincing matters, he rapped, 'Very well. You can hear it from here.'

And while she was wondering what in creation he was talking about he snarled, 'Leave Geoff Rogers alone!'

Her jaw dropped. Scandalised, she stared at him. So stunned was she by what he had just tossed at her, she didn't react for a moment. 'Leave him alone?' she finally echoed.

'I knew it was a mistake to have a female cluttering up the board,' he grated.

Anger arrived, and she was glad of it. Overbearing chauvinist pig! 'Forgive me for not being one of the chaps!' she retaliated hotly, and was ignored for her trouble.

Ashlyn weathered Carter's icy look—clearly he wasn't used to tart-tongued women. 'You realise that Rogers is married?' he charged equally acidly.

So what had that got to do with the price of carrots? 'We didn't discuss his wife!' Ashlyn snapped waspishly.

'I'll bet you didn't!' Oh, for a meat-cleaver! 'Stay away from him!' Carter Hamilton ordered shortly. 'I'm not having the Hamilton name linked with some sex-scandal hitting the headlines!'

My God! His *nerve*, his unmitigated *nerve*! Ashlyn was so flamingly angry with him that she came close to thumping his head. Right there, outside a restaurant frequented by quite a number of newsworthy patrons, she came close to physically attacking him.

Somehow, however, she managed to find a grain of control. But it was with all the vitriol at her command that she tautly replied, 'Then I suggest, Mr Hamilton, that you curtail your own sexual activities!'

And with that she managed, by supreme effort, to do what she should have done some sixty seconds ago—she turned smartly about and stormed away from him.

All she knew then, as she marched rigid-backed down the street, was that if she hadn't found the control to walk away from Carter there would have been a very real risk of her giving the headline writers something else to write about. Something like BOARD MEMBER OF HAMILTON HOLDINGS SAVAGES CHAIRMAN! Never had she met such a man who could throw her so out of gear emotionally! Loathsome brute!

CHAPTER THREE

IT TOOK quite some time before Ashlyn came down from the pinnacle of her outrage. She had never hit anyone in her life—but it had been a near thing. He might be the chairman, she fumed as she drove home, but up until his 'Leave Geoff Rogers alone!' speech Carter Hamilton had barely said two words to her— she wished he'd kept it that way! Making her sound like some over-sexed trollop! Oh, how she wished she *had* thumped him!

She was about two miles away from her home when a streak of fairness pushed its unwanted way into her thoughts. So, OK, he was the chairman, and no head of any concern would welcome a scandal, would they? Indeed, wouldn't any chairman worthy of the title nip anything untoward in the bud, so to speak, at the first suspicion that damage might be caused to the firm he had worked so hard for?

To blazes with being fair, though. This man wanted her out—off the board. Was this the start of him trying to get rid of her?

Ashlyn was both defeated and angry at the same time. Then, as she turned into the gates of her home, she saw her father taking his ease on a garden seat. She had known in advance that he would want her to tell him everything—how on earth was she going to do that?

How, when her father set such store by her being on the board of Hamilton Holdings, could she tell him—leaving out the water episode—that she had been warned off one of the other board members? How, when he had such pride, could she tell him how she had come close to landing one on the chairman—which would have been guaranteed to get her thrown off the board? Oh, what a total disaster the day had been!

As she'd expected, her father was halfway across the lawn as she got out of her car. 'How did it go?' He didn't wait until he was up close to ask.

She could not lie to him, but found it impossible to tell him the truth. 'Different,' she hedged. 'It was different.'

'I expect it would be different from what you're used to,' he agreed a trifle impatiently. 'But how did you get on? Were they all there?'

If there had been any more they'd have had to find another leaf for the boardroom table!

'I think so. Sixteen of us and a PA taking down the minutes.' Oh, Lord, those minutes! She dreaded to think how her water fiasco would look in print. 'People had flown in from all over. Though not everyone came to lunch with us.'

'You had lunch with some of the directors?' Her father looked impressed.

Feeling as if she had just escaped a very tricky situation, Ashlyn explained, 'We entertained two very nice Americans to lunch, and—'

'How many were you?'

'Our two guests, and six others.'

'But not Carter Hamilton?'

I wish! 'Yes, he was there...'

'Really!' Her father was impressed—and she could not, for the sake of his pride, and hers, tell him the rest of it.

And he was proud. She later heard him talking on the phone to one of his brothers, telling him what a busy morning she'd had at her board meeting. 'Carter Hamilton insisted that she join a few of them for lunch afterwards,' she heard him say, and was heartily glad he hadn't been there to see Carter Hamilton's hostile expression when Geoff Rogers had

asked her to join them. Oh, if only Carter's
arrogance hadn't pricked her into accepting!

She was at breakfast on Friday morning
when the post arrived. Her father brought it
into the breakfast room, but instead of taking
his chair and sifting through his mail as he normally did he remained standing, a considering
look on his face as he studied one envelope in
particular.

'It's for you.' He looked up to address her
and continued, handing the envelope over, 'It's
got the Hamilton Holdings crest on it.'

Oh, no—those wretched minutes! Now what
did she do? 'You realise that—er—everything
at that meeting I went to on Tuesday was confidential,' she said in a rush—she who had
barely understood one word of it.

Her father looked disappointed that she was
not going to share with him the business under
discussion. But then he brightened and looked
proud again. 'I'm glad to hear you appreciate
that,' he stated without protest, and she was
proud of him.

But although he wasn't expecting her to show
him what was in her letter he still clearly expected her to slit open the envelope and take
out its contents. She had hoped to read the
minutes in her room.

With a sinking feeling, Ashlyn tore the envelope and, on taking a nervous peep inside, was mystified that instead of there being typewritten matter enclosed there was a cheque, and a compliments slip.

'It's a cheque!' she told her father, her spirits dipping, not knowing the first thing about how one was dismissed from a board, but wondering if this was some sort of severance pay.

'That'll be your attendance fee,' he answered knowledgeably.

'Attendance fee!' She blinked, couldn't believe it, and just had to smile. 'You mean I get paid for going?'

'Naturally. I'd be most surprised if you didn't.'

'Wow! My first wages!'

She at first thought it funny, then thought it great—and then fell to earth with a guilty bump as she realised how little she had done to earn it. And those accursed minutes were still hanging over her head!

Ashlyn went out with her friend Susannah Veasey over the weekend. But, close friend that Susannah was, somehow Ashlyn felt unable to give her a blow-by-blow account of her entry into the world of big business last Tuesday.

Susannah knew that she had been to the board meeting, though, and wanted to know, 'Is Carter Hamilton as dishy in the flesh as he looks in the newspapers?'

Ashlyn had instant recall of what Carter Hamilton looked like. In fact the insufferable man, and his insufferable, good-looking face, had returned to haunt her constantly since she'd had the misfortune to meet him.

'In a word, yes,' she replied, as in all honesty she had to.

'Fancy him?' Susannah asked.

She'd sooner fancy a gorilla! 'Not my type,' Ashlyn answered casually—and spent the next week—when she wasn't thinking about what a swine Carter Hamilton was—wondering what man was her type.

Oh, she had dated. Could have dated more, she supposed. Perhaps the fact that she had six male cousins, was comfortable in male company, and certainly was neither intrigued nor fazed by any of the opposite sex, had made her dates more friend material, than boyfriend material.

Oh, she'd been kissed and had kissed back, but little more than that. She sometimes wondered if she was a bit staid—a few of her friends had relationships. But somehow going to bed with any of the men she knew was something she had never felt was necessary to be a complete being.

She had many friends who were male, and was exceedingly fond of Todd Pilkington, but she'd be embarrassed to death if he made a pass of any sort at her. And he, she was certain, felt likewise.

So, what was her type? she couldn't help wondering that week. And why wouldn't Carter Hamilton clear off out of her head? She didn't like him, never would—so why did she waste so much time seeing his face, his expression, and going through everything over and over again?

Another week passed, and by the following week Ashlyn was on an even keel again, and had realised that Carter need not have got up from the table to open the boardroom door for her the way he had done. Perhaps, noticing her discomfiture, the gentleman in him had got to work. Somebody had kindly sent Ivy too—had it been him?

Ashlyn was back to seeing nothing gentlemanly in his behaviour, however, when a few days later her father handed her another envelope bearing the Hamilton Holdings crest.

'The minutes, I expect,' she said lightly—it was a far thicker package than the last one. 'I—um...' She wanted to take it away upstairs. But to do so seemed mean—even if she did feel dreadful. 'I'd—er—better open it.'

'Would you like my paper knife?'

'This will do,' she answered, taking up a knife by the side of her plate.

Having slit open the envelope, she extracted its contents, and noted that she had also been sent an agenda for the next meeting. But she was far more interested in the minutes of the last one.

Hoping her recent penchant for changing colour from pale to scarlet had been a mere phase, Ashlyn quickly scanned the gobbledegook until she came to the part she was so desperately interested in. She felt she'd never survive the embarrassment if every board member read of her aquatic performance. They had been there, of course, but would they treat it as so deadly confidential as she did, or would they tell all and sundry?

She felt quite sick inside when she spotted it right there, in between the lawyer entering the boardroom and leaving. Oh, thank goodness! It could have been so much worse. Much, much worse than the brief notation: 'Miss Ainsworth was indisposed and left the meeting'.

'Interesting?'

Ashlyn looked up. She had forgotten her father was sitting there. 'Absorbing,' she answered, and quickly shuffled the papers, putting the minutes to the back and the agenda to the front. 'There's another meeting next Tuesday,' she commented, relief rushing in on two counts: despite Carter Hamilton's threatening statement that 'the minutes should make some very interesting reading', the part she had played in the meeting had been dealt with in a very few words. Also, her father, respecting her remark about the meeting being confidential, had not asked to see the minutes. But her relief was short-lived.

'Ten o'clock, as before?' he enquired, and Ashlyn, realising he was asking about the next board meeting, knew without question that he fully expected her to attend.

She studied the papers in her hands. 'Eleven,' she answered, and changed her mind about going just for the sheer hell of it. 'It looks as though it will be a shorter meeting than the other one.' And she added, with her limited knowledge of such matters, 'It doesn't look so important either.'

'Some are, some aren't,' her father commented. 'If it's to be a shorter meeting, though, I don't suppose there'll be as many there as last time.'

Ashlyn perked up—even if she still wasn't going. 'You mean Carter Hamilton might not be there?' Not that she was afraid of him, for goodness' sake; the man just sort of disturbed her, that was all. She hadn't known she had such a want-to-kick-his-shins kind of temper before she'd come across him.

'He doesn't have to attend every meeting,' her father stated. 'He's a very busy man, so will most certainly have a second in command to stand in for him.'

Ashlyn remembered Bill Trevitt saying how Fitz Unger was his deputy, and supposed that every chairman had one. 'If he's not going, then perhaps I needn't...er...' Her voice petered out at her father's sudden and abrupt sharp look.

'I hope you're not thinking of letting me down, Ashlyn!' he rebuked her sternly.

She gave an inner sigh but, looking at her father, she remembered how hard he had worked all his life, how he had seen to it that she and her mother had nothing but the best, and she began to feel exceedingly mean. He had laboured long and hard—all he was asking of her was that she do this job for him. A job that amounted to only a few hours a month. For goodness' sake, only *two* hours next time, if they started at eleven and finished at one. And, with luck, *he* wouldn't be there on this occasion.

'Of course I wouldn't let you down!' she denied brightly, and, leaving her chair, she went over and gave him a kiss, and then took the agenda and the minutes up to her room.

Half an hour later, she was amazed to realise that after reading through the minutes several times they started to make sense! Chunks of that boardroom meeting played back in her mind, and the mumbo-jumbo, now that it was set down concisely and she had studied it, took shape and began to have meaning.

Ashlyn didn't know who was responsible for translating the matters under discussion into something intelligible—Carter Hamilton or his PA—but she felt very much cheered that, business-wise, perhaps she wasn't so dim after all. Who knew, given a little training—well, quite a lot actually—she might be able to contribute something?

The thought amused her. Not at that high-up level, she wouldn't! Grief—it was only because her father had stuck out for it that she'd been allowed through the hallowed portals of the boardroom anyway. And, as her father had said, if she didn't do anything they could hardly remove her from the board. Bearing in mind her father's 'I hope you're not thinking of letting me down', just now she knew that, for his sake, while Carter Hamilton might do everything in his power to get her legally removed, she was going to stick it out and stay there—come what may.

Which was why, the following Tuesday, dressed in a greeny-blue two-piece and with her shining red hair once more in a classic knot, Ashlyn said goodbye to her parents and drove off to Hamilton Holdings.

She owned to having butterflies in her tummy, but she had determined on waking that morning that she was going to think positive. So what if she had come close to belting Carter Hamilton at their last meeting? Thinking positively meant he wouldn't be at this one. Furthermore, for him to have approved those minutes he must have read them *after* their set-to outside that restaurant. He might, for all she knew, have instructed his PA that the commotion she had caused was to be set down merely as Miss Ainsworth having left the meeting because she was indisposed.

Ashlyn parked her car at Hamilton Holdings, got into the lift and pressed the top-floor button. Perhaps, despite his warning her off Geoff Rogers, Carter was a gentleman after all.

She recognised two doors on the top floor: one that led to the ante-room and to the boardroom, and one to the ladies' cloakroom. She nipped into the cloakroom to check her appearance—hair still all right, no long wisps anywhere. Lipstick fine. She squared her shoulders. Think positive! she told herself, and headed for the boardroom.

'Ashlyn!' Geoff Rogers, at least, was pleased to see her, and, although her determination to be positive wobbled a fraction, she was glad to see him—a friendly face.

'How are you?' she enquired, walking towards him.

'You know that you're beautiful, of course,' he uttered quietly in a 'just the two of us' tone, meeting her halfway and taking her right hand. But, instead of giving her a handshake, he held her fast.

She laughed—what else could she do? He was a flirt. He was obvious. But he was also friendly, and she couldn't see anyone else breaking their neck to rush over and say hello.

The door behind her opened. She half turned—and her stomach somersaulted. The last time she'd seen Carter Hamilton, he'd bluntly told her to leave Geoff Rogers alone. She saw Carter's glance skim over her. Oh, great! He looked through her; that 'you don't exist' look said it all! Carter Hamilton was not happy to have come into the room to find her laughing and holding hands with the very man he had warned her off!

Ashlyn was still reminding herself to think positive when a general move was made towards the boardroom. Everyone seemed to know their place. Positive thinking. She chose to go to the seat she'd used the last time she'd been there—she was grateful to see that either by luck or someone's hard work there was no water mark visible on the highly polished table to remind her of her last visit.

'Good morning...' And so the meeting began.

Ashlyn did not drift off so much this time. Indeed, she found some bits of the business under discussion quite interesting. But during the parts that weren't—and when Carter wasn't speaking—some of the other high-powered executives had the most wearying, droning voices. However, she was determined that even if she did feel like nodding off her hands were not going anywhere near that water carafe.

She glanced around—and suddenly met Carter Hamilton's gaze full-on. Crazily, her heart fluttered. His expression was, as ever, unsmiling—yet he had such a good-looking face. Grief! What was the matter with her? Abruptly she looked away.

'And that concludes...' someone was saying, and the meeting was wound up.

As her heart's rhythm returned to normal, Ashlyn realised that the meeting was over, and that she had not disgraced herself. She began to feel better. Once a month! Child's play!

People began putting their papers together, standing up, making a move towards the door. For some odd reason, Ashlyn found she was hanging back. Somehow she just didn't want to be within range of Carter Hamilton. She wondered what had got into her; for goodness' sake, she wasn't afraid of him; he couldn't hurt her! But she still hung back. She was within hearing range when one of the board asked if Carter was lunching with them.

She saw Carter shake his head. 'I'm lunching elsewhere,' she heard him reply, and felt a most peculiar sensation as she translated it to mean that he had a lunchtime date with one of the elegant, not to mention beautiful women she had seen him pictured with in the newspapers.

He then disappeared from view, and Geoff Rogers was by her side. 'You're coming with us, aren't you, Ashlyn?' he asked.

She usually had a good appetite, and was fortunate in being able to eat anything she fancied without adding an ounce to her slender shape. Yet strangely she just didn't feel hungry now.

'Do you mind if I don't?'

He did. 'I insist,' he wheedled.

She laughed. Whatever he was, he was obvious, but she liked him. 'I've some shopping...' she began vaguely.

'I won't take no for an answer,' he returned stubbornly as they went through the ante-room and into the corridor.

Someone wandered between them. Ashlyn, who had no intention of having a 'Yes, you can, No, I can't' argument in the lift, took off for the other door she recognised on that floor.

Ten minutes later, she judged it safe to leave the ladies' room. She was walking back along the corridor, thinking about what she could and could not recount to her father when she got home, when she saw another door up ahead open. A moment later a mature, well-built man appeared, followed by Carter Hamilton.

Oh, heck. Why she should want to turn about and go the other way Ashlyn had no idea. But, if she didn't want to look foolish, she would have to go on. Which would mean, since this must be the man that Carter was lunching with—not one of his lady-loves as she had imagined—that they would all be going down in the same lift.

Carter was closing the door just as she reached them. Ashlyn went to walk on by, but to her surprise, not to say astonishment, she felt her arm caught and held in a firm grip. Made to halt by Carter, she turned, and, letting go of her arm, he addressed his companion.

'Osmund, I'd like you to meet our newest board member, Ashlyn Ainsworth.' Ashlyn guessed she was still in shock. Carter, for a change, was not ignoring her but was actually introducing her. She stood where she was and even extended her right hand to the man as her chairman completed, 'Ashlyn, this is Mr Kogstad who's over from Oslo to see us.'

Mr Kogstad was Norwegian! She loved Norway! She smiled a welcoming smile. *'Det gleder meg å hilse på Dem, Herr Kogstad.'* She

shook hands with him, aware that Carter
Hamilton was doing something of a double
take. Norwegian wasn't her best language, but
from the beaming expression on Herr Kogstad's
face she guessed her greeting of 'I'm pleased to
meet you' had been received and understood.

'You speak my language!' Herr Kogstad exclaimed warmly.

'A little,' she owned modestly, thinking that
since it didn't appear as if Carter spoke
Norwegian, and that since Osmund Kogstad
obviously spoke English, it would be better to
continue in the latter.

'Your accent is perfect,' Herr Kogstad assured her, and gallantly asked, 'You are joining
us for lunch, perhaps, Ashlyn?'

No way. She opened her mouth ready to
make her excuses. 'Actually I've arranged—'
But she got cut off before she could invent anything very clever.

'Everyone wants to take Ashlyn to lunch,'
Carter Hamilton sliced in pleasantly, and
Ashlyn turned to stare at him. His tone might
be even, but there was a steely glint in his eyes.
Still in the same pleasant tone, her chairman
went on, 'But we have priority over everyone
else.'

She couldn't believe what she was hearing! Was he saying that he wanted her to lunch with them? Was he pulling rank, ordering her to break her other arrangement...? Ah. Click. Suddenly it dawned on her that he thought her other arrangement was to have lunch *à deux* with Geoff Rogers.

She smiled. It offended her to be bossed about by Carter, but since she was certain that it was only out of duty to the group's good name that he was ordering her to lunch with them—and that personally he would hate it like poison—she could afford to be magnanimous.

'I'd love to have lunch with you, if I may,' she beamed. She felt it might sound insincere if she told Herr Kogstad how she truly loved his country, and so said instead, 'It's some while since I was last in Oslo—I should like to hear of any changes to your capital.' You swine, Carter Hamilton, she fumed, and wondered how, with so much dislike in her soul for one man, she could, at the same time, smile and chat so pleasantly to the other. She'd just love to tell Carter that with his efforts to stop her having lunch with Geoff he had spiked no one's guns but his own!

Yet, even while she disliked Carter Hamilton like crazy, even while she was aware that the feeling was mutual, as they progressed from lift to car to restaurant she just knew instinctively that Carter would do and say nothing in front of their guest that would make her look small.

And so she relaxed. Herr Kogstad was Carter's guest at lunch, and, because of her connection with Hamilton Holdings, the Norwegian was her guest too. 'I hope you're hungry, Herr Kogstad?' she enquired. Since something light was never going to fill either man's large frame, she added, 'I believe the peppered steak here is quite splendid.'

'This restaurant is a favourite of yours, Ashlyn?' Carter pressed suavely.

She'd been once—and was saving up before she came again. 'Lord, yes,' she answered blithely, and was happy to be consulted by their guest who needed some item on the menu translating into Norwegian.

She was hungry suddenly, and ate well, glad that the other two did also. Over the meal, at their guest's request, she fell to calling Osmund by his first name too.

'Does the funicular still run there?' she asked him when the port of Bergen was mentioned, and soon they were deep in discussion.

'You sound as if you visited my country often, Ashlyn,' Osmund commented.

'Not recently, I'm afraid. But my parents and I went every year for a skiing holiday for a while.'

And so it was a pleasant lunchtime. Though Ashlyn was at pains not to hog the conversation, and felt perfectly at ease sitting back when Carter had anything to say, she was a little astounded at quite how charming he was to her. He brought her in, as well as their guest, to comment when the occasion demanded it—not that she trusted Carter for a moment. He'd be looking through her again at the next board meeting; that she didn't doubt.

To her surprise, she discovered that for all this lunch could be called a working one business was barely touched upon. She acknowledged she had a lot to learn.

'That was a marvellous meal,' Osmund thanked Carter as they left the restaurant, and, turning to Ashlyn, he said, 'I will bring you here the next time I come to England.'

Carter wasn't the only one with charm, she observed. 'I should like that,' she smiled.

'Are you coming back to the office with us, Ashlyn?' Carter enquired.

For the second time she declined his offer of a lift back to Hamilton Holdings. 'If you'll excuse me,' she answered nicely, 'I've one or two bits of shopping...'

She shook hands with Osmund who sincerely insisted that if she was in Oslo before he was again in London she must contact him and his wife and they would be delighted to entertain her. Ashlyn went on her way wondering why she hadn't gone back with the two men. It had never been her intention to do any shopping. Yet she felt that she wanted to be on her own. It was almost as if she felt that being in Carter Hamilton's company for too long was unnerving. How ridiculous!

As she had thought, her father wanted to know all that she could tell him as soon as she arrived home. Both he and her mother were in the drawing room, and he was voicing his first enquiry as she walked in through the door.

'How did you get on?'

'Very well,' she assured him—after all, she had understood a little of the meeting this time, so that had to be a vast improvement!

'Who was there?' Before she could answer, another question came. 'Carter Hamilton wasn't there?'

'He was, actually. He chaired the meeting.'

'Well, he would,' her father stated, as if that much was obvious. 'Er—you're a little late— did you go out to lunch again?'

'Mmm—I did have lunch,' Ashlyn answered. She didn't know why, but she felt she would prefer to leave the matter there.

'Who with?' her mother, whose antenna had tuned into something worth investigating, asked.

'Um—Mr Hamilton was entertaining a Norwegian businessman. They kindly invited me along and—'

'Did they now!' Her mother and father exchanged glances. 'Other board members were present?'

'Well—no.'

'Just the three of you?'

'Yes,' Ashlyn reluctantly owned—and knew then why she had not wanted to say with whom she had lunched. She wouldn't put it past her father, or her mother either, for that matter, to be on the phone to one of her uncles within the next half an hour to exaggerate the importance of her presence at the lunch.

Ashlyn knew it for a fact on Friday evening, when she met up with her cousin Duncan for a drink. 'What's this my mother tells me about you being one of the most popular members on the board of Hamilton Holdings?' he teased.

'No!' she gasped.

'Ah,' he grinned. 'Methinks it comes under the same heading as "Of course, Duncan's tutors think he's the most brilliant student they've ever had".'

She had to laugh; his mimicry of his mother's voice was superb. 'Shut up, and mine's a gin and tonic,' she told him.

The weekend seemed to be particularly dull. In fact Ashlyn got up on Monday morning and realised that she felt restless, with a need to be doing something. But doing what? She found no answer. All she knew was that ever since she had returned home last Tuesday she had felt that there was something—something inde-finable—lacking in her life.

And yet as far as she could remember she hadn't found the board meeting so overpow-eringly stimulating. She'd been pleased to have understood more of what was going on, of course, but even so there had been great chunks of it that remained a mystery to her.

Perhaps speaking with Osmund Kogstad had revived memories of the wonderful holidays she and her parents had spent in Norway. But why should that make her feel restless now?

Ashlyn was still feeling much the same around midday. Both her parents were out, just she and the housekeeper at home, when the phone rang. 'I'll get it!' she called to Mrs North. She had meant to give Todd a ring—it was probably him now.

'Hello,' she said.

'Hello, Ashlyn,' answered a voice that was male, but was not Todd's. A voice which she instantly knew; why did she feel the need to sit down? 'Carter Hamilton,' the voice announced.

'Oh, yes,' she answered warily. He had been pleasant to her the last time she had seen him, but they'd had a guest with them. She must never lose sight of the fact that Carter Hamilton was looking for a way to remove her from the board.

'I've a problem,' he stated.

She almost said 'Oh, yes' again, but changed it to a cagey, 'A problem?' From what she had seen of him, Carter could handle any problem standing on his head!

'The thing is, Lorna Stokes, my PA, had an accident over the weekend . . .'

'Oh, I'm sorry!' Ashlyn exclaimed spontaneously. She remembered his PA. A very pleasant, capable-looking woman. 'Is she . . .?'

'She's not too badly hurt, but she's in plaster and will be in hospital for a while. She'll be off for some weeks after that until her bones heal.'

'Oh, the poor woman.'

'What about poor me?'

Selfish brute! If you want a little sympathy, come to me—I've got as little as anybody! 'What about you?'

'I'm without my most efficient and all but indispensable PA.'

The poor woman could probably do with a rest. 'So where do I come in? Good grief!' she exclaimed, quite without thinking. 'You don't want me to be your PA?'

Even as her temporarily departed brain matter returned to acknowledge her question as ludicrous, Carter was asking—sarcastically, she was sure—'Can you type?'

Rat! 'What's that got to do with anything?' Ashlyn bridled. She heard a muffled sound at the other end of the phone, and if she hadn't known him better she'd have suspected Carter of covering a laugh—as if she'd amused him. But she'd rarely seen him smile, so doubted very much that he had a sense of humour, much less one that was on a par with her own.

'In point of fact, I've got other staff covering most of Lorna's PA duties—that isn't where the problem lies.'

'Oh?' Ashlyn queried politely.

'Where I need more specialised help is with the public relations side of her work.'

Ashlyn had no intention of rushing in with another impulsive, brainless assumption. 'I'm not with you,' she said.

'You, Ashlyn, whether you know it or not, are a natural on the PR side.' He was complimenting her on something? The moon would be blue tonight!

'What are you asking?' she asked as she started to recover.

'Just that you come in and be ready to chat to people when I'm not available.' Feeling slightly staggered, at the same time Ashlyn started to feel more perky as Carter went on to outline, 'Lorna knows all the people I deal with. But, in her absence, an associate or board member of another company is going to feel much more valued if they're put through to a member of our board, rather than having to speak to someone covering my PA's duties. Don't you agree?'

She did. Having attended a couple of board meetings where business worth millions was discussed, she saw the sense of a VIP being put through to a board member, rather than being asked to leave a message with whoever happened to be in the PA's office at that time.

'Well, yes,' she had to confess. 'But—' She broke off. She had almost said, But I know nothing about the business, and at once realised the mistake of that. She realised she knew nothing, and thought this man must know it too; he wanted her off the board, but for her parents' sake she had to stay there. No way was she going to give Carter Hamilton ammunition which he could use later. Suddenly, startlingly, it dawned on her that this might be a trap.

'Well?' Carter's tone was short. This she judged, was a man who was unused to asking anyone for anything.

And, if it was a trap, surely she could find the ins and outs of his PA's 'accident' once she took on her phone-manning position? Yet she hesitated to accept, though there was a part of her, a part she did not understand, that was very keen to take on the job.

'Er—it would entail my coming in every day—Monday to Friday?' she queried.

'That's when we do business!'

Pig! 'But...' She paused, smiled to herself, and asked prettily, 'Aren't you worried that if

I come in every day I might bump into Geoffrey Rogers?'

There was a silence at Carter's end. She guessed her query hadn't helped him to swallow the fact that he'd had to ask her for something—and realised that there were better and much sweeter ways of getting even for some slighting remark than thumping someone. She was really enjoying this!

'You—want me to apologise for what I said.'

On your *knees*! 'A small grovel wouldn't come amiss!' she replied—and definitely heard a laugh, brief though it was. But she did not get her apology.

'Are you coming or not?' he barked.

And *she* wanted to laugh. She didn't really need an apology. Carter must have rethought his opinion of her behaviour with Geoff Rogers, or he would not be offering her this job now. And she no longer felt restless, she felt stimulated, and knew that, for however long this job might last, she wanted it.

'Do I get my own desk?'

'You get your own office.'

It got better and better. 'When do I start?'

'As soon as you can.'

Ashlyn took a deep and steadying breath. 'I'll be in tomorrow!' she said—and put down her phone receiver.

She almost punched the air, she felt so happy.

CHAPTER FOUR

ASHLYN'S euphoria had evaporated somewhat by the following morning, when, with both her parents up and around to wave her off, she set out for Hamilton Holdings.

She must have been carried away by the confidence Carter Hamilton had that she could do the job, she realised, because this morning she was sure that she could not.

That would not stop her from giving it her best shot, though, for several reasons. One: Carter would be forever on the lookout to give her a black mark for something. Two: her father, and her mother too, to a lesser extent, had been at first incredulous, and then jubilant, when she had told them about her new, temporary role. And three: she now had to make a good showing, if only to save her father's face—because her uncle Richard had dropped in last night. He'd barely been across the threshold before her father had been telling him how Carter Hamilton had phoned her in person that day.

83

How she'd managed to cover her dismay when she'd heard her father tell his brother, 'So Ashlyn's no longer a mere non-executive member of the board but an executive director,' she did not know. The trouble was, even though her father was getting so carried away, her loyalty to him meant there was nothing she could do or say to contradict him.

The nearer she drove to Hamilton Holdings, however, the more Ashlyn worried about how she was going to cope, and deal with the chairman. A month ago she would have said he could go hang before she would help him out. So, given that she had accepted the job, and without too much deliberation either, did that mean she did not dislike the man so much as she had thought?

Ashlyn arrived at Hamilton Holdings, parked her car, and, her insides in uproar, took the lift to the reception area. An assistant named Una was waiting for her when she stepped out. 'Miss Ainsworth?' Una enquired, her eyes on Ashlyn's classic knot of thick red hair, as if she had been advised that the person she was looking for would have hair of that colour.

Ashlyn, very much aware of her lack of training and business knowledge, was quite surprised when Una, explaining that she had been roped in to help in Mr Hamilton's office, showed her to the office she had been allocated. Ashlyn discovered she was to be housed on the top floor—with all the other high-ranking executives.

Her office was airy, spacious and the one nearest the lift and stairs. 'Is this all right for you?' Una enquired. 'Mr Hamilton said if you—'

'It's fine,' Ashlyn smiled. It was more than fine; by her reckoning, she was only going to be here for a month or so—less if she blotted her copy book and Carter found a way of getting her off the board. But this was an office which any executive would be delighted to have. 'Er—how's Mr Hamilton's PA—do you know?' she enquired, following up thoughts that having her under his nose might be Carter's way of finding some weakness he could use—and that perhaps Lorna wasn't so badly injured, maybe even not injured at all.

'It looks as if Lorna might be in hospital a little longer than we at first thought,' Una stated. 'Mr Hamilton went to see her last night and learned the doctors may have to reset her leg.'

It sounded ghastly! And, having dubbed Carter as being unsympathetic to his PA, Ashlyn revised her opinion. It had been kind of him to go to the hospital to see her—though, on second thoughts, he'd probably used his visit to clear up any business he needed to know about.

Una left her to go back to her own domain and Ashlyn spent five minutes testing her chair, opening drawers and checking the view from her window. The sound of her door opening caused her to spin round. Briefcase in hand, Carter Hamilton entered.

Ridiculously, her heart fluttered. 'Just coming in?' she asked, having realised from Una's remarks that he must have arrived some while ago, but, oddly, feeling the need to pass some sort of off-the-cuff remark.

'Just going out,' he answered casually. 'Got everything you need?'

'Telephone, notepad, pencil,' she documented the tools of her trade, all there on her desk.

'You're staying till five?'

He hadn't mentioned office hours—but she was still wary of being trapped. 'Of course,' she answered.

'Good!' His glance roved over her dainty features, then rested on her wide green eyes. 'I'll look in when I get back.'

Ashlyn subsided into her chair once Carter had gone. He was, she owned, quite something! And as he had to pass her office every time he wanted to use the lift or the stairs she supposed she must get used to him popping in. It was only natural that he would want to find out if there were any messages for him. After all, message-taker-in-chief was her role.

Her office was conveniently situated for anyone else to drop in too if they felt like it, she found, when less than an hour later Geoff Rogers stopped by.

'Just heard on the bush telegraph that you're delighting us with your presence,' he beamed with a charm born of long practice.

She was pleased to see him. 'Carter thought I might be useful,' she smiled.

'What's your job title exactly?' He settled himself in a spare chair near her desk.

'I don't know that I've got one,' she laughed. 'It's just that as Lorna Stokes is in hospital I might be useful in taking calls from anyone who particularly wants Carter.'

'What a brilliant idea. I say, my PA's gone down with this flu thing—you wouldn't care to

take mine too, would you? I'm off out myself
in half an hour.'

'I'd be pleased to,' she answered truthfully.

'Lovely girl—have lunch with me tomorrow?'

'You never miss an opportunity,' she
laughed. 'No.'

'Can't hang a man for trying.'

Ashlyn felt cheered after he'd gone, but had
still not taken any calls when, at eleven,
someone brought her a cup of coffee. A short
while after that Ivy, whom she remembered
warmly, tapped on her door and came in
wheeling a trolley.

'I've had a message from Mr Rogers,' she
stated cheerfully. 'He tells me you've joined us
as Director of Senior Communications and, as
such, will need coffee-and tea-making facilities.' While Ashlyn didn't know whether to
gasp or laugh at Geoff's inventive 'Director of
Senior Communications', Ivy was busily un-
loading from her trolley a hot plate, china, and
the refreshments which Geoff had decided she
needed.

Ivy chatted on, saying she would get a small
table sent up, then just as cheerfully, went on
her way. Ashlyn worked out that she could well

find herself entertaining Geoff to tea or coffee whenever he passed by.

It was a little before twelve when Ashlyn took her first call—from Italy. Signor Vezio Morini wanted to speak with Carter.

'*Buongiorno*, Signor Morini,' she greeted him. Someone in Carter's office had already explained to him that Carter was unavailable but that he was being put through to another board member. '*Posso aiutaria?*' She asked if could help him.

'You speak my language!' he exclaimed, sounded youngish and excited, and there followed a full five minutes of Italian conversation. Signor Morini left a message which meant little to Ashlyn, but she recorded it and put it to one side. The Italian then got down to other interests. 'Would you like to fax me a picture of yourself?' he requested.

'I'm afraid I don't have one,' she laughed.

'But you are under thirty, yes?'

'Yes,' she replied, realising she was being flirted with. But she had no wish to be churlish—that was not part of her brief.

Eventually Signor Morini said goodbye and Ashlyn smiled. She had liked him. Looking down at the message she had taken, she felt useful, and liked that too.

She took another couple of messages after that, both for Geoff Rogers, and went out to lunch feeling in no way taxed but somehow enjoying the feeling of being more involved with Hamilton Holdings.

The first hour after lunch seemed to drag by, then she heard the lift stop, heard footsteps that halted by her door. She looked up to see that Carter Hamilton was back.

'Ah, a message for you,' she smiled, and glanced down to pick up the note which she had translated from Italian. She looked up to find that Carter was gazing at her hair with almost a hint of admiration. Her heart gave an idiotic kind of flip.

'Do you always wear your hair that way?' he asked, the question seeming to come from him involuntarily.

'Only when there's an R in the month,' she replied smartly, and could have sworn she saw his lips twitch.

She was mistaken, she realised a moment later. For there was not a scrap of good humour about him when he glanced over to the table and its accompaniments, which hadn't been there the last time he'd been in this office. 'I see you've made yourself at home,' he drawled, and she could have hit him—and Geoff Rogers for his hand in making it look as if she was setting up a canteen.

'I'd offer you a cup, but I know you're busy,' she forced out a smile.

He grunted something—she was sure it was something uncomplimentary—and, taking her hint along with his message, he strode off.

Ashlyn felt strangely as if she'd just been pulled through a wringer. Never had she met a man who could so upset her equilibrium—and so easily at that.

'Any chance of a cup of tea?' Geoff Rogers asked when he steamed in at just after four o'clock. And, perhaps reading her expression which said 'No chance', he added, 'I've been stuck in traffic for the best part of an hour.' Ashlyn relented. Why shouldn't she give him a cup of tea? She hoped Carter Hamilton came by and caught them. See what you get for being pleasant!

On Friday of that week, Ashlyn added another board member to her list of people for whom she took messages and did a bit of PR. Henry Whitmore's PA rang her. 'I've a Mr Yates on the line. He's angry that Mr Whitmore hasn't returned his call and now Mr Whitmore isn't in—can you help?'

A dozen questions flew into Ashlyn's head. Was he just cross about not having his call returned, or did he have some bigger gripe? 'When will Mr Whitmore be in?' she asked.

'Not until after lunch.'

Having received that information, Ashlyn could not see the sense in asking what the caller's business might be, since any technical jargon was going to fox her completely. In her view the angry Mr Yates was not going to be made much sweeter by being kept waiting any longer.

'Would you like to put him through?' she requested, fully sympathising with Mr Yates because it didn't sound as though Henry Whitmore was treating him very well. 'Good morning, Mr Yates,' she greeted in warm tones. 'I'm sorry you're having trouble contacting Henry. I wonder if I can help in any way?'

'You're on the board of Hamilton Holdings, Whitmore's secretary tells me.' Oh, my word— he did sound angry.

'That's right, and liking it tremendously,' she answered enthusiastically, only then realising that, for all she had been by no means stretched since Tuesday, she had enjoyed coming to Hamilton Holdings. 'I still have a great deal to learn, of course.'

'You know nothing at all about my company, do you?' Mr Yates questioned. Ashlyn realised then that she had two choices: admit it and put down the phone, or...

Suddenly she remembered the day she had lunched with Carter and Osmund Kogstad, when hardly a word about business had been uttered, and in she plunged. 'I'm hoping to rectify that as soon as possible. I wonder, Mr Yates—are you free for lunch today?'

He hadn't been expecting that; she could tell from the sudden silence at the other end of the phone. 'You want to take me to lunch?' he checked, but sounded much less angry than he had been.

'If you're free,' she replied warmly, not allowing herself to think.

'Well, that'll be a first,' he answered, and she guessed he meant this was the first time he'd had a business lunch invitation from a female of the species—did she have news for him! 'Where and what time?' he accepted.

The only place that came to mind in the flurry of the moment was the restaurant where Carter had entertained Osmund. She gave the name and suggested midday, keeping her fingers crossed that, by taking an early lunch, she might be able to get a table.

She was on the telephone again to the restaurant shortly after she had said goodbye to
Mr Yates, still not allowing herself to think
of the enormity of what she was doing. She
knew absolutely nothing about business, for
goodness' sake! She did the only thing
possible in her efforts to secure a table; it
was unthinkable that she ring Mr Yates back
and tell him that their venue had been
changed to somewhere more lowly. 'Good
morning,' she greeted, 'I'm Ashlyn Ainsworth;
I'm a director...' Director of Senior
Communications—ye gods! '...with Hamilton
Holdings. I wonder if you've a table for two
available at lunchtime?'

'Today?'

Grief, she could hear him saying 'Not a
prayer' already. 'Around midday?' she
ploughed on, adding quickly, and hating herself
for using Carter's name, 'I lunched with you a
week ago last Tuesday—I was with my
chairman, Carter Hamilton...'

'Oh, Mr Hamilton! Um—around midday,
you say?'

'Twelve noon,' she confirmed—and put
down the phone grinning wildly. So who was
to know?

She soon lost her grin; panic set in as Ashlyn realised that while this lunch was not arranged for her to discuss business—and hallelujah for that—if Mr Yates started to get in the slightest technical as he told her about *his* business he was soon going to discover that she had not the smallest concept of what he was talking about. He would then begin to wonder what on earth she was doing on the Hamilton Holdings board. Oh, dear, she hoped he didn't know Carter. Or, if he did, that the two never met.

The fates were working for and against her that day. On the for side, Donald Yates turned out to be a slim, mid-forties, fair-haired male. His anger with Henry Whitmore over, he was tickled to be entertained to lunch, and could not have been more pleasant. As for her worry that the talk about his business might be too technical, as they chatted through lunch he seemed content to give her a brief outline of what his company did.

'I've a daughter about your age,' he revealed over coffee. 'She's just finishing at university. Rosie wants to come into the firm. What do you think? Should I let her?'

'What do you want?' Ashlyn asked, knowing her own father's views on a daughter entering his business.

Donald, as he now was to her, gave a huge soppy grin. 'I'd love it,' he said. Ashlyn was grinning in empathy, when she looked up straight into the cool, dark, not-very-pleased-to-see-her eyes of Carter Hamilton.

'Ashlyn,' Carter acknowledged her.

'Carter,' she replied. Her insides were all of a jangle—as fates went, they couldn't get more against than that he'd chosen to lunch here—but, never knowing quite how, she kept her outward poise. 'Donald, do you know my chairm—?'

'Hello, Carter.' Donald Yates took over and, as relaxed as you please, said, 'Are you joining us?'

The fact that Ashlyn and Donald were on their coffee and would shortly leave was not lost on Carter. 'I'm lunching with someone,' he replied urbanely, and, switching his glance to Ashlyn, he asked, 'Are you going straight back to the office?'

'Yes,' she replied, sensing she was in his black books for something, but not wanting Donald Yates to know it.

'You might tell my office I'll be late back.'

'No problem,' she answered, and irritatingly found herself wondering who he was lunching with that would make him 'late back'. Some female, no doubt!

She did not get to find out because Carter moved off to go and greet his guest. Then she had her attention taken up with a mild battle because Donald Yates would not allow her to pay for the meal.

'But I invited you!' she protested.

'I know. And I wish I could let you pay. But there's just something in me that can't allow you to sign the bill with everyone else looking on.'

'How about I do it in private?'

He shook his head, and charmingly made her giggle when he said, 'You wait until I tell my wife that I lunched with an absolutely gorgeous redhead—and that *she* wanted to pay!'

Back at her office, Ashlyn phoned Carter's office with the message that he would be late back. 'We know. He said,' she was informed, and Ashlyn put down her phone thinking it odd that Carter had forgotten he had already informed his staff. And a few minutes later Carter was still in her head; had he not forgotten at all, but just wanted to know if she was spending the afternoon with Donald—or if she intended going back to her office?

Nosy devil! she fumed, and felt cross with him, reminding herself yet again that this man wanted rid of her, and was forever on the lookout for a way of doing it. Carter had caught her consorting with the enemy, perhaps? But Hamilton Holdings did business with Donald's firm, so he couldn't be called the enemy. Ashlyn gave up that particular line of thinking but resolved to be constantly vigilant where Carter Hamilton was concerned.

At half past three, Ashlyn blinked, came to, and realised that she had been staring into space ever since she had come back from lunch. She got up, put on the percolator and rang Henry Whitmore's office, thinking that perhaps she should chat with him about her lunchtime session with his client.

'He's on his way to see you,' his PA informed her, and less than a minute later a mature man she remembered from the two board meetings she'd attended came in with a huge bouquet of flowers.

'What did you do to Donald Yates?' he asked. 'He was charming when I rang to beg forgiveness for my sins.'

Ashlyn smiled, and thought Henry Whitmore a very nice man as he presented her with the bouquet. She had a coffee with him, while they discussed the few bits and pieces which she considered relevant for him to know.

At a little before five, with not one single call having come her way that afternoon, Ashlyn, her flowers in one arm, picked up her bag and left her office. She was standing looking at her flowers as she waited for the lift and thinking pleasantly how nice everyone at Hamilton Holdings was, when it arrived.

She looked up; the lift doors opened. She moved forward, then took a step back. Some time to come back from lunch! she thought tartly as Carter Hamilton stared from her to the beautiful flowers she carried, then back to her face—and without the smallest acknowledgement walked from the lift and straight by.

Ashlyn marched into the lift and banged the 'Parking' button. Correction. How nice everyone at Hamilton Holdings was, bar one!

'What lovely flowers!' her mother exclaimed when she arrived home. 'They're gift-wrapped!' she observed.

There was no escaping the question that was bound to come next. 'One of the directors gave them to me,' Ashlyn felt forced to reply. And because she didn't want her mother to think there was any romantic interest there she added, 'For—a job he thought I'd done—er—all right.' She could have groaned as soon as the words were out. Before the evening was over, her simple reply was going to be embroidered upon, she knew it. By the time she went to bed, both Uncle Edward and Uncle Richard would know how excellent she was at her job. Now did not seem to be the time to tell her mother that the chairman wasn't speaking to her—that he'd looked through her rather than acknowledge her. Perhaps his lunch hadn't been so appetising after all! One could only hope.

Ashlyn spent some of the weekend with her friends Todd and Susannah, and thought of them with affection on Monday when, alone in her office, she sat waiting for her phone to ring. Tomorrow, she decided, she would bring a book to read.

On Tuesday, however, the phone on her desk rang several times. Once in connection with Carter—who was out of the country for a week, she'd learned. Twice for Geoff Rogers. Once for Henry Whitmore, and once—word having got around, apparently—for another board member, Mr Joseph Fulford.

Ashlyn decided to take a look around and find out from which office every resident board member worked. She discovered that Carter preferred to work in isolation and that his team of assistants were housed in an office across the corridor from him.

To investigate where everyone worked seemed to her, with her knowledge of board members increasing, to be the efficient thing to do. Even if Geoff always seemed to stop by for a chat whenever he came in.

So why did she feel down today? Was it the fact that she was enjoying her role at Hamilton Holdings, underworked though she might be, and she did not want to leave? She had known from the start that the job was only temporary!

Or did she feel so flat because she would *not* be bumping into Carter that week? Good heavens, how ridiculous! What in creation had put that thought into her head? As if she were missing him—she was missing him like a sore tooth!

Ashlyn promptly pulled herself together and pushed him from her thoughts, and, as her phone rang again, discovered that she was not as underworked as she had thought.

In fact, by five on Friday, she realised, with the exception of Monday, she had spent a busy week. The world and his wife seemed to have dropped by for either tea or coffee, and her phone had been earning its keep. She had met Joseph Fulford, and had remembered his face from the board meetings she had attended. He was another charming man, which still made her feel that everyone at Hamilton Holdings was nice—bar one. But she had decided not to think about *him*!

Oddly, that weekend seemed to be kind of lacklustre. Indeed, it was a pleasure to get back to her office on Monday—even if her job was only temporary. And she had never felt more alive when, late that afternoon, Carter stopped by her office.

'Anything I should know about?' he enquired, dark eyes taking in her smartly clad person and resting on her pale, translucent skin.

'Vezio Morini rang,' she informed him, thinking no man had the right to be as good-looking as Carter, and so self-assured with it. 'He—'

'Business or pleasure?'

Halted by his question, Ashlyn stared at him from wide green eyes. 'It's always a pleasure to speak with Vezio,' she stated mildly, wondering what it was about this man that could instantly cause her hackles to rise. 'But in this instance—'

'Vezio?'

'He asked me to use his first name. But—'

'He tells me you speak Italian like a native.'

'One tries,' she shrugged, realising that of course the Italian had been in personal contact with Carter since that first call she had taken from him. But she was getting rather fed up with Carter Hamilton. 'Look—do you want his message or not?' she snapped.

'If you can deliver it without the flowery bits!' Carter grunted, seeming to know that, with Vezio getting personal, the call had taken three times as long as it should have.

Ashlyn handed over the paper with the relevant details. 'Nice to have you back,' she murmured pithily—and nearly went into heart failure when, just before he took the paper from her and turned about, she definitely saw the corners of his splendid mouth twitch. Good heavens, her acid had amused him!

She was still coming to terms with the astonishing fact that Carter Hamilton had a sense of humour the next morning, when she received a very humourless call from someone the company dealt with, who thought he had been treated very shabbily.

Her information was scant, save knowing that the man's name was Philip Corbett. Since he had been put through to her straight from the switchboard, she had no clue which board member normally dealt with him.

'It's not good enough!' he complained. 'Anyone would think you don't want my business, the way I've been treated.'

'Oh, I'm sure it's not that at all, Mr Corbett,' Ashlyn assured him. She had no idea what his business was, but felt certain that they were going to lose him if she didn't do something about it. 'Are you free for lunch?' she heard herself enquire before she could think about it.

By lunchtime she had been through a whole welter of should she, shouldn't shes. And because most people on the top floor were occupied with other business that day, she had not been able to trace who Philip Corbett's contact at Hamilton's was.

She left her office to go and meet him, unable to see what else she could do. Plainly he felt slighted. So in the interests of making him feel better— Dammit, she was a board member, wasn't she?

Ashlyn owned that her confidence had grown and grown since that day she had invited Donald Yates to lunch—and that meal had gone excellently. Donald had been a charming man.

Philip Corbett was not a charming man. He turned out to be the type of man with whom she had nothing in common—and there was definitely something about him which she did not take to.

But if one did business only with the people one liked then one wouldn't get very far. So, having invited him to an expensive but different restaurant from the one where she had lunched with Donald Yates—she somehow did not want to risk seeing Carter again—she smiled whenever she could, and did her best to placate Philip Corbett.

'Every company has an overdraft,' he explained petulantly. 'And naturally my credit's as good as the next man's.'

'Of course,' she offered gently, not knowing the first thing about it.

'But, with Hamilton Holdings issuing instructions to Dowell Pneumatics—one of your companies, as you know—not to renew my contract, I'm about to go under—lose my firm that I've worked so hard to build up.'

'That would be dreadful,' she agreed, and started to feel extremely sorry for him. He reminded her of her father. Oh, not in manner by any means, but like her father this man had toiled all hours. Despite her father's hard work, he had lost his firm—even if he had been handsomely compensated—and it seemed a

point of honour to her that Philip Corbett
should not lose his.

'If you'll leave it with me, I'm sure we'll be
able to work something out,' she smiled, still
not liking him any better, but sympathising with
his predicament.

'Perhaps we can meet again?' he suggested,
his shifty eyes making a meal of her bosom.

She felt uncomfortable and her sympathy
dipped—she dragged it up again. 'I'll phone
you to let you know what I've been able to arrange,' she smiled.

'I didn't mean meet to discuss business,' he
leered—and Ashlyn couldn't pay the bill fast
enough.

Managing to avoid all further innuendo, she
was greatly relieved to leave the restaurant.
'We'll be in touch as soon as we possibly can,'
she promised, and, hailing a taxi, she saw him
into it.

She summoned another taxi for herself,
having half decided that never again was she
going to take a client of Hamilton Holdings out
to lunch.

By the time she had reached her office,
however, she was already starting to change her
mind. So, fair enough, she hadn't enjoyed this
particular lunchtime, but it had never been part

of her brief to enjoy herself, had it? Her job
was to make clients who were on the boards of
other companies feel valued when the people
they wanted to speak with weren't around.

In actual fact—she caught herself up
short—her brief was to do that job for
Carter—the other board members at Hamilton
Holdings had just sort of crept in. As, she
realised, taking her chair behind her desk and
thinking about it, Philip Corbett had crept in.
Only then did she see that he was not on any
board of any company that Hamilton Holdings
dealt with per se. But, as the owner of a
business, he had decided he wasn't getting anywhere with Dowell Pneumatics, so had con-
tacted their parent company.

As her father would have done, Philip
Corbett had gone to the top. The fact that he
had got her was not going to be his misfortune,
she determined, and started to feel angry on his
behalf. She wished someone had been there to
smooth over things for her father. Picking up
her phone, she consulted her list of internal
numbers and stabbed out a few digits.

'Yes!'

Grief, Carter didn't sound too ap-
proachable! 'Are you busy?' she asked. Oh,
Lord, what a stupid question. He'd just got

back from a week away—of course he was busy! She felt inadequate, and that made her even more angry. 'Can I come and see you?' she asked shortly.

'You'd better come now before you explode!'

The line went dead. Swine! So why did she take out her compact and check that she looked all right? Oh, for heaven's sake. Impatient with herself, impatient with him, Ashlyn was halfway to Carter's office before she realised that he hadn't asked who she was. But, as if he already knew, and was certainly aware that she was cross about something, he had said, 'You'd better come now before you explode!'

She had never been inside his office before. But not many seconds later she was tapping on his door, and, not waiting to be invited, she entered a very large, airy room. As well as housing office furnishings, it also held several sofas and chairs. She supposed it could be less formal than the boardroom, should Carter want a friendly conference with any of the people he dealt with.

But she was not there to admire the decor, and noted that Carter had risen to his feet as she went in.

'Take a seat, Ashlyn,' he invited calmly, his dark eyes seeming to penetrate her very soul.

'This won't take long,' she replied, her eyes going to the mound of complicated-looking paperwork on his desk. She took a hard chair; her legs were suddenly feeling a little bit shaky. She was glad that Carter resumed his own seat. But it was without saying a word; his eyes were watchful and he waited for her to continue. 'I've just had lunch with a man called Philip Corbett,' she began, and knew at once when Carter frowned that he knew of him.

'He's a friend?' he enquired shortly.

'I'd never met him before today,' she answered, a touch snappily. 'He rang and was put through to me. H—'

'He invited you to lunch?'

She was telling this, not Carter! '*I* invited *him*,' she corrected, and could see straight away from the firming of Carter's mouth that he thought she had overstepped the mark. Well, she didn't care—something had to be done for the man.

'That's part of your job, is it?'

'*You* do it!' she countered. 'You entertain people we do business with. I was with you that day—'

Her argument got lost when, slicing across what she was saying, and as sharp as a tack with his assumptions, he interjected, 'Did you invite Donald Yates out the other Friday too?'

'Well, yes, I did,' she owned. And, for Donald's sake, felt she had to further confess, 'Only he wouldn't let me pay.' And, finding she had been issued with the most diabolical conscience—one she definitely did not want—she then blurted out, 'I used your name to get a table.'

He was not impressed. He grunted and then snarled, 'You know he's married!'

'Philip C——?'

'Yates—Donald Yates!' he corrected her sharply.

My stars, he was the most annoying, difficult... 'And has a daughter my age!' she snapped.

'How old are you?'

She'd thought he knew everything! Surprise, surprise! 'Twenty-two. Look, we're getting away from the point!'

'The point being that you feel, as a member of my board, that you can take out to lunch anybody you please.'

'You appointed me PR *extraordinaire*!' she flashed back, her green eyes sparking.

Carter stared at her, his eyes taking in the pale pink of anger tinging her cheeks, before his glance steadied on her eyes. 'You said it,' he drawled, and she was sure he was mocking her—and that made her madder than ever.

'Why are Dowell Pneumatics refusing to renew his contract?' she challenged on a splutter of outrage.

'For one—his company's going bust.'

'Well, of course it is!' she flew. 'If we're not willing to...' Her voice faded when she saw from the slight narrowing of Carter's eyes that he wasn't taking too kindly to having decisions which had been made at top level queried. Her anger started to ebb—perhaps she was being impertinent. Then she thought of her father— even if he had ended up most financially sound. 'Couldn't we—couldn't we reconsider?' she asked.

Carter was already shaking his head. 'We're talking millions here, Ashlyn,' he told her evenly. 'But, that apart, the man's a crook. We want nothing more to do with him.'

'He's a crook?' she queried, her eyes going saucer-wide.

'I've had him investigated. Trust me. We've made the right decision. Dowell Pneumatics made a grave error of judgement in ever dealing with him.'

'Oh,' she gasped, more glad than ever of the chair beneath her.

She thought Carter's look softened a little, but was mistaken, she knew, because he was hard through to the core. That much was evidenced in his cool, 'Might I suggest that in future you're more careful about whom you take to lunch?' Ashlyn glared at him, realising she had just had her wrist slapped. She didn't like it, and felt she hated him. She was totally unprepared for the alert intelligence in his eyes and his sharp words when he abruptly challenged, 'He asked for a date, didn't he?'

'What if he did?' she retorted, still smarting from Carter's rebuke, and finding that she refused to take any more.

'So he did!' he snarled, and went barking on, 'I assume he knows we do business from the boardroom, not the bedroom!'

Instantly Ashlyn was on her feet. She wanted to slit Carter's throat! He was standing too when, so angry that she didn't know how she stopped herself from launching herself over the desk at him, 'For your information, Hamilton,' she blazed, 'I don't—'

'Not on the first date?' He seemed furious too, and hell-bent on going for her jugular.

'Nor on the tenth!' she retorted, acting on fury, not brain power.

She only realised how unthinking she'd been, how goaded by him she had become, and what she had revealed, when, as sharp as ever with his calculations, all fury went from him and Carter exclaimed, 'Good God! You're a virgin!'

He was quick—too quick! She hated him some more. 'What's wrong with that?' she challenged, her chin tilted defiantly.

Carter surveyed her silently for some moments, but only to remark mildly, 'No need to be defensive about it.'

'I am *not being* defensive!' she flew back, flustered, maddened, and hating the sound of her voice rising.

He looked deep into her eyes, then his glance moved down to her mouth. 'Those eyes, that mouth say you're not frigid, so don't worry about—'

He was the *limit*! 'I'm not worried about anything!' she shrieked. His *nerve*! His... Words failed her. She calmed down an iota— was she really standing here having this conversation? And with *him*? 'Oh, stuff it!' she erupted, and did what she should have done a full minute ago. She spun about and got out of there.

Ashlyn was still fuming five minutes later. Pig, pig, double pig! Ye gods, what was it about that man? She played back in her mind the conversation she'd had with him and she still didn't believe the last part of it. His diabolical nerve! 'Don't worry about—' Who the hell did he think he was—some comforting agony uncle? Swine! That'd be the day when she went to him for advice. Though, when it did come to *that* sort of thing, without a doubt he was an expert!

Abruptly Ashlyn turned her thoughts away. Thinking of him and his women gave her a peculiar sensation in the pit of her stomach. She concentrated instead on the first part of their conversation.

By the sound of it, Philip Corbett's company had been thoroughly investigated, found to be up to no good, and any business dealings had been immediately terminated. Hamilton's, as she was coming to know, would not touch anything that was not one hundred per cent above board.

So where did that leave her? She had been reprimanded when Carter had told her to be more careful whom she took to lunch in future. But he hadn't told her to leave, or thrown her off the board. Was that being fair-minded on his part, or was he waiting for her to make a more concrete kind of mistake before he told her, Oh, dear, what a shame—byee?

An hour later, Ashlyn had started to worry that, even though Philip Corbett had deliberately misled her by not giving her the full facts concerning his dealings with them, she nevertheless had given him a promise that they would be in touch soon—and that promise would have to be broken.

She toyed briefly with the idea of sending him a personal note to the effect that her efforts had proved fruitless—but against that she did not know whether anything she wrote might count against her.

In fact, she realised hopelessly, in spite of her confidence having boomed in the two weeks she had been at Hamilton Holdings, she still knew less than nothing—about anything.

Having been furiously angry, with her adrenalin soaring, Ashlyn was on the edge of hitting the deepest trough of despair when the phone on her desk rang. It was the switchboard. 'A Mr Todd Pilkington is on the line. He says it's personal. Will you take the call, Miss Ainsworth?'

Her spirits lifted. 'Oh, yes, please,' she replied. 'Todd! How are you?' she smiled down the phone when they were connected.

'Wish I'd got that kind of welcome from the girl I tried to date last night!' Todd answered, and Ashlyn laughed—and at that precise moment her office door opened and Carter Hamilton came in. Her smile died; Todd was still talking, but she heard not a word. Carter's expression was as unsmiling as ever—she guessed that either she was in trouble again or Carter had been out and, as he was passing, had looked in to see if she'd taken any calls on his behalf. 'So Susannah said she wasn't keen, but that she'd go if you'd go.' Ashlyn flicked her glance away from Carter and tuned in again to Todd.

'Er—sorry, Todd. Did you mean tonight?' she queried, realising that some of the group were going somewhere and that Todd was doing the organising.

'Of course tonight! I'll pick you up at eight. Just say yes, and I'll get back to Susannah.'

'Eight, tonight,' she repeated, her wits slightly scattered. 'Yes, I'd love to.' She made herself concentrate—difficult with Carter standing there glowering and waiting impatiently for her to finish what was so obviously a personal call. 'I'll look forward to it,' she smiled—and replaced the receiver with no idea about what she had committed herself to.

'Anything for me?' Carter questioned grimly before she could draw another breath—plainly he was a man disinclined to wait another moment.

'Nothing!' she answered in kind, and weathered his arctic look. But, just as he turned to the door, she found her conscience getting the better of her. 'Er...' He halted, turned, stern-faced, and waited for her to continue. The words wouldn't come. At least, not until he raised his left hand and deliberately looked at the watch on his wrist. Diabolical swine! One of these days... 'I promised Philip Corbett we'd be in touch as soon as we possibly could,' she stated flatly.

Carter's look was none the warmer, and she guessed he thought she had a fine nerve committing the company's promise to a crook like Corbett. But, if he thought it, he didn't say it. Instead he stated curtly, 'I'll take care of it.'

And that was that. Her head ached. She didn't want to go out that night—and she had not the foggiest notion of where she was going.

When five o'clock came, so did a telephone call that was to delay her from going home. It was from a man she had spoken to before, who had an urgent message for Joseph Fulford. 'It's in connection with something most confidential he's working on. But it's vital he has this information before the start of business tomorrow. Well before, if he's to have any chance to sort through his strategy. I'd have rung earlier, but I've only just got the bare facts myself. Can you help?'

'No problem,' she assured him. She took down his message, made little sense of it, repeated it back for accuracy and, armed with her notes, she went along the corridor to Joseph's office.

Joseph Fulford was not there, but she hadn't expected him to be. Why else would she take his messages? Disturbingly, though, neither was his PA. Clearly she'd better things to do of a Tuesday evening at ten past five than to hang about the Hamilton Holdings building.

Now what? Ashlyn went back through to Joseph's office again. Glancing at his desk, she saw his PA had tucked a note into his blotter where he would see it when he came in. It was a non-essential kind of note but pretty obviously he was expected back that evening.

Ashlyn toyed with the idea of tucking her note into the same blotter. She dismissed it. I her information was vital and so confidential, she had better hand it to him personally. He'd probably look in in a minute.

At five forty-five, Ashlyn was still thinking the same—though not with the same conviction. At ten to six, she tried to raise the switchboard. As she had thought, the switchboard operator had plugged in an outside line—and gone home. An outside line. Ashlyn smiled. Perhaps Joseph had decided not to return to the office and had gone home too. She would ring him. Problem solved.

A few minutes of searching for his phone number soon showed she still had a problem. Two, in actual fact, if you counted that she had to get home herself and be ready to go out by eight o'clock.

She left Joseph's office and called at all the other offices on the top floor—bar one. Everybody else had gone, it seemed. She remembered the mound of paperwork she had seen on Carter Hamilton's desk. She had been to his office once today and didn't want to go in again. But since she understood he worked late each evening he was her only hope.

He *was* still there. He looked up as she went in, his expression no warmer than it had been the last time she had seen him. 'Do you have

Joseph Fulford's home telephone number?' she asked bluntly.

'What do you need it for?'

A yes or a no would have done! 'I've a message for him,' she replied shortly.

'You take messages for him?' He seemed surprised. Then he took a moment out to recall, 'You lunched one of Henry Whitmore's associates too.' Bluntly he added, 'What's going on?'

'*Nothing's* going on!' she denied heatedly. Honestly—this man!

He was waiting—wanting more. Which was why she decided he could take a running jump before she'd tell him more. Only, she still wanted Joseph Fulford's home telephone number. It was an impasse and she knew it. And she had to be home and ready by eight.

'If you must know, word has spread that while Lorna Stokes is off sick, your calls are switched to me when you're out. I occasionally do the same thing for one or two of the other board members.'

'The hell you do!'

She wasn't sure if he was admiring, annoyed—or what he was. 'I'm hardly stretched,' was the best defence she could come up with.

'But anyway, I've taken this message for Joseph...'

'He's not coming back tonight.'

She'd gathered that much herself! She tried hard to keep calm. 'Well, anyway, it seems pretty vital that I contact him. Do you have his home phone number?'

Carter stared at her levelly for long seconds, his good-looking face expressionless. Then, not looking in the least regretful, he replied suavely, 'What a pity—I don't. He's just had his number changed and hasn't thought to let me have it.'

Blow that for a tale! Why she felt sure he was lying she couldn't have said. 'But this message is obviously important,' she insisted, and, moving closer to his desk, she handed Carter the details of the call.

'There's no mistaking that,' he agreed, handing the piece of paper back. 'He'll have to have that information before morning.' Ashlyn had no belief at all in the hint of a smile that crossed Carter's expression as he volunteered, 'I do have Joseph's address, though.' And, picking up his pen, he wrote it down and handed it to her, instructing, 'You'd better drive over and deliver it in person.'

Ashlyn looked at the address and saw that Joseph lived in an entirely opposite direction from where she lived. 'But I don't live anywhere near...' she began to protest. Dammit, she was sure Carter knew Joseph's phone number. 'Anyway, I've got a date tonight!' she further protested, hoping perhaps that Carter might be more reasonable.

Fat chance! 'It's tough at the top!' he drawled. Miserable toad! He looked quite cheered that she might have to break her date!

'You don't live anywhere near?' she hinted—and saw him smile for the first time.

It was a mistake to believe in that smile too, and Ashlyn could have hit him when, not sounding in the least unhappy about it, Carter informed her, 'Would that I could go for you—but I've a heavy date myself tonight.'

Ashlyn felt that peculiar sensation in the pit of her stomach again—and hated him some more. 'I hope you enjoy it!' she snapped, hoping nothing of the sort—she prayed his date gave him rabies.

'Oh, I will,' he assured her silkily.

Ashlyn slammed out to go and phone Todd. Rat, rat, double-dyed rat!

CHAPTER FIVE

BECAUSE it was now known that she was a board member, Ashlyn had no trouble the next morning when she visited each PA on the top floor and entered their director's home address and phone number in her diary. In the event of anything similar to last night's performance happening again, she had no intention of having to go to Carter Hamilton for that sort of detail.

She was still cross with him, and still convinced he had been lying when he'd said he hadn't got Joseph Fulford's home number. He was just too efficient, just too—everything not to have it. Though why he had withheld that number from her she couldn't decide. She whittled it down to two possibilities: either he was testing her to see if she had the company's interests sufficiently at heart to let them take precedence over her private life, or he was just being bloody-minded and did not care that she'd had to break her date.

Not that going out with Todd and the gang could in strict terms be called a date. But *he* wasn't to know that. Pig!

It was around ten o'clock when the man at the top of her detestation parade strolled into her office. 'Find Joseph all right?' he enquired pleasantly.

'Yes, thank you,' she answered prettily, and because she couldn't resist it added, 'And my date waited for me.' She didn't see why Carter Hamilton should have the sole prerogative of lying.

'Don't forget the board meeting next Tuesday!' he answered crisply.

Love you too, she silently fumed. And so the day progressed. And the next, and the next. And Ashlyn, her humour restored, drove home on Friday evening realising that she had been fully occupied these last three days. Her job seemed to have grown!

It still slightly amazed her that, while knowing nothing at all about business, she could talk so confidently with highly influential people. But it appeared that she could, because one or two of them asked especially for her when they phoned.

Top-floor executives seemed, just lately, to be forever dropping by *en route* to their own offices. And yesterday Henry Whitmore had called on her lunchtime services to go with him to help him entertain a couple of associates.

'You've got a Cheshire cat grin all over your face!' her mother remarked when she went in. 'Had a good day?'

'You could say that!' Ashlyn answered, smiling, and felt so good about being a part of the working scene, she stooped and gave her mother a kiss.

'Don't forget to tell your uncle Edward all about it at his retirement dinner tomorrow night!' her mother called after her as Ashlyn headed for her room. Her parents were still suffering from this pride thing, then!

Ashlyn loved her family, and enjoyed family gatherings. Her uncle Edward's retirement dinner was no exception. The following evening she went with her parents to join her six cousins, their wives and older offspring to celebrate with her other uncles and aunts the eldest Ainsworth's well-earned retirement.

It was a happy party, but, as ever, one proud parent after the other seemed to be bursting to relate some clever, endearing or amusing anecdote regarding their progeny.

Her father's opportunity came during the main course, and Ashlyn was stunned, not to say mortified, to hear him proudly boast, apropos of almost totally nothing, 'Of course Ashlyn is invited to other board members' homes now.'

All eyes turned to her and she felt absolutely unable to humiliate her father by stating that she had merely been delivering a message to one of them. She had no option but to look modestly down at her plate as if fascinated by the King Edward potato thereon.

'You're doing well, I hear, Ashlyn,' Teddy, another of her super cousins, commented lightly.

'Not bad,' she answered—and discovered that reply was not good enough for her mother.

'Not *bad*!' she exclaimed. 'You should have seen her face when she came home yesterday. She's taken to her business career as if born to it.'

'Being an executive director can't be easy,' her uncle Richard opined, and Ashlyn, dying a thousand deaths, was grateful when her cousin Duncan, who was sitting next to her, gave her elbow a nudge.

'Go with the flow, coz,' he muttered, as if aware of her high embarrassment. 'My folks are only waiting for yours to shut up so they can get started on telling one and all of my masterly intellect.'

Ashlyn was cheered, and he was right. She guessed that all families were like that as Duncan's praises were sung. Perhaps her parents weren't any more proud than the rest of the family. Though when she recalled that it was because of her parents' pride that she was doing her 'executive director's' job in the first place she doubted that.

Geoff Rogers' PA, who'd had a dreadful and prolonged bout of flu, returned to work on Monday, but Ashlyn discovered that she was still fielding calls for Geoff.

'You don't mind, do you?' he enquired, always the flirt although, having discovered Ashlyn wasn't playing, he had toned it down a little. 'It will give Elsa a little time to catch up.'

'I don't mind at all,' Ashlyn replied, ever aware that, even if this job had grown to be full-time, it would come to an end when Lorna Stokes returned.

Ashlyn saw nothing of Carter that day, and went home that night looking forward to the board meeting the next day. Oh, not because she would see him there. Perish the thought! It was just that she had found the last meeting more interesting than the previous one. And, now that she knew a little more—true, not a great deal more—it should be most interesting listening as matters slipped into context.

Ashlyn drove to Hamilton Holdings on Tuesday hardly able to believe how much she had changed in the space of less than three months. To begin with she had been terrified at the prospect of attending a board meeting. Yet here she was today, actually looking *forward* to it!

Carter was not at the meeting. 'Good morning, everyone.' Joseph Fulford took the chair and opened the meeting with Carter's apologies for not being there. He was, it seemed, away on other business.

And the meeting was deadly dull. Ashlyn wondered why she had ever looked forward to it. She knew the names of everyone there now, and several of them had greeted her in the ante-room, Henry Whitmore in particular breaking off from what he was saying to call, 'Don't run away afterwards, Ashlyn. I need your help.'

She kept herself awake throughout the meeting by wondering what he wanted her help with. But, much though she liked Joseph, he had a sleep-inducing voice. Carter, now, he... Grief, she was actually comparing the man favourably with someone! 'Out, damned spot!'

In this case, a Gloucester Old Spot, a breed of pig she must have heard about from somewhere or other.

'Coming to lunch with us, Ashlyn?' Geoff Rogers came over the moment the meeting was over.

She was about to accept when Henry Whitmore came over. 'My need is greater than yours,' he said as he edged Geoff out of the way. 'Ashlyn and I have been invited to lunch with some people we met last week.'

'They've invited me?' Ashlyn asked in surprise.

'They insist that you come along,' Henry informed her.

Ashlyn started to feel better. Henry might be gallantly stretching the truth a little, but it did her heart good that she had been included at all. It made her feel a true part of the team.

She had another pleasant surprise on Thursday afternoon when her office door opened and a man of about thirty came in. He was dark-haired, olive-skinned—and was dramatically distraught.

'*Mamma mia!*' he exclaimed, on seeing her. 'I am just on my way back to Italy and thought I must find a moment to go and see Ashlyn of the beautiful voice—and here you are—enchanting!'

Ashlyn left her chair to go and shake hands with him. 'How nice to meet you, Vezio,' she greeted him, for he could be no other than Vezio Morini.

'Ah, you are so beautiful—and you know who I am!'

He was, to say the least, a little over the top, in her opinion. But she could not help but like him. 'Of course,' she smiled, and, falling naturally into her hostess mode, asked, 'Have you time for tea or coffee before your flight?'

'I should have called on you first and let my other business wait,' he mourned. Somehow, while making him a cup of tea, and for all he spoke excellent English, they fell to speaking Italian.

And then it was time for him to rush off. 'Have a good flight,' she bade him.

Vezio took both her hands in his and, despite the fact that he barely knew her, he kissed both her cheeks. 'Next time I am in London, I will call on you first,' he stated. '*Arrivederci*, my beautiful Ashlyn.'

She collapsed onto her seat when he had gone. Vezio Morini had charm by the cartload. Yet, for no reason she could think of, a man came to mind whose charm was conspicuous by its absence when he was talking to her. She guessed Vezio had been to see him. Carter must have told him where to find her.

Geoff Rogers, late in and in a rush the next morning, stopped by her office on the way to his own. 'I'm lunching with some people today—it could be heavy going. Be an angel and come with me.'

Was she the boardroom's PR liaison officer and message-taker-in-chief or wasn't she? 'If you think I'll be any help,' she agreed.

'Oh, you will be,' he beamed. 'I don't know what it is, or how you do it, Ashlyn, but people relax around you.'

'I've already agreed to come,' she teased.

'No soft soap, honest!' he assured her, consulted his watch and rushed off.

Lunch was a pleasant affair, and Ashlyn didn't know what Geoff had worried about. True, there was more talk about business than when she had lunched with Carter, or Henry Whitmore for that matter. The conversation brought forth moments when she judged it best not to try to contribute. But there were other times when a word here and there seemed to be the nudge needed to keep things flowing.

And if the length of time they'd taken over lunch had made the occasion fruitful, then the fact that it had gone four by the time she returned to her office also seemed to hint that it had not been unsuccessful.

Ashlyn returned to her office, switched on the coffee-maker and made a mental note to tell Mrs North not to cook her an evening meal in future. These business lunches were starting to become regular. However, she reminded herself, this would not go on for very much longer. Lorna Stokes was now out of hospital. Soon Carter would tell her that her job was over.

That thought saddened her. She didn't want to leave. It had been a big adjustment leaving home daily to do her nine-to-five stint, but she had adapted far more easily than she would have believed. And, for all she could not have said what exactly it was that she did, and she felt that she could hardly call it hard work, she did not want it to end.

Just then, her door opened. Looking so tight-lipped that she would not have been surprised if he had told her this was her last day with Hamilton Holdings, Carter came in.

Her heart started to pound, pound so much that she realised she must want to stay on at the company more than she had realised.

'Kind of you to come back!' Carter grunted by way of openers. How to win friends and influence people!

'I've been out to lunch!' she flared. She might want to hold onto her job for as long as she could, but she didn't have to sit meekly and take everything he threw. 'It was business!'

'Business?' he echoed, his eyes on her alert. 'Business for this company?'

'As it happens, yes. Geoff Rogers and—'

'You've been out to lunch, all this while, with Rogers?'

'And enjoyed it very much!' she retorted defiantly. 'And before you start,' she charged on, never having forgotten he had warned her against involving the Hamilton name in some sex-scandal that very first day she had met him, 'Geoff Rogers is harmless.' When he looked likely to interrupt, she added, 'We didn't lunch cosily on our own, if that's what you're thinking, but with a Mr Foster and a Mr Ison.'

That surprised him. He swayed back a little anyway, his expression suddenly more speculative than angry. 'You had lunch with Foster and Ison?'

'And very enjoyable it was too!'

'Was it?'

'Shouldn't it have been?' she countered, and wished he would either go or sit down. He was tall, and seemed to dominate her office. And she wasn't going to be dominated by him or anyone else!

Carter regarded her for silent moments. 'Foster and Ison aren't generally known for being full of the joys,' he commented after a while. Ashlyn tried hard to hide that she knew someone who would make up a good joyless threesome. She realised she hadn't quite made it, and that Carter must have read her mind, when he enquired, 'Did anyone ever tell you that you have very expressive eyes?'

Oddly, she wanted to laugh. But she wouldn't! 'So, what did you want to see me about?' she asked. 'Or did you just come in to have a go at me?'

'Were you intending to have a cup of coffee?' he enquired.

Was he asking for a cup? 'Have a seat,' she invited. He did just that, lowering his long length onto her 'guest's' chair.

Quickly, efficiently, while wondering what she was doing—he was bound to stay another five minutes now—she poured him a cup, found out he liked his coffee black and sugarless, and handed it to him.

'So?' she encouraged as she sat down behind her desk. If he had come to have a go at her perhaps it would be over in less than five minutes.

'So?' he queried back. Was that some quirk of amusement trying to pucker up the corners of his mouth? She didn't believe it!

'So what else did I do to earn your wrath?'

'Are you always this blunt?'

She shook her head. 'To be honest, no. But I've an idea you'd see through anything I tried to dress up.'

'You honour me.' His tone was slightly mocking but, instead of it making her cross, Ashlyn, to her bewilderment, felt she wanted to smile again. 'So tell me, who else, when they're not dropping in here for tea or coffee...' so he'd heard about the other board members on this floor? '...steals you away to lunch when they've got a tricky assignment?'

'I don't know about tricky assignments,' she replied, but saw no reason not to be open. 'I've lunched with Henry and some clients once or twice. Although the last time,' she added, wanting to be absolutely fair, 'Henry's associates kindly invited me along.'

Carter scrutinised her, his glance travelling from her smooth, unlined forehead, down over her dainty nose, to play around her mouth, her chin and long, slender throat, and then, after taking in her coil of superb red hair on the way back, his eyes met her green eyes—and held them steady.

After another two or three long moments of studied silence, he drawled, 'Are you trying to make yourself indispensable?' Highly unlikely though it seemed, she somehow knew that Carter Hamilton was teasing.

She could hardly believe it. Carter—teasing? Teasing *her*? She stared at him, her green eyes wide. And, needing suddenly to say something, she asked, 'Talking of indispensable, how's Lorna?' And immediately wished that she had not. Because if he had come purposely to tell her that this was her last day with Hamilton's she had just given him a splendid opportunity to do so!

But much to her relief he said nothing of the kind, and answered, 'She's doing very well— though she won't be back as soon as both of us hoped.'

Ashlyn started to feel guilty that she was happy his highly efficient PA would not be back yet, and settled for the comment, 'She'll be glad she's out of hospital.'

'So,' Carter began, having spoken suffi- ciently about his PA, it seemed, 'not only are you busy most of your day disarming tele- phone callers and taking messages for all and sundry on this floor, but—'

'Did you mean me to work exclusively for you?' she tried to interrupt.

'But, soothing furrowed brows with tea and coffee along the way, you also allow yourself to be used as a buffer at business lunches.'

Ashlyn didn't quite see it like that. However, for once, all discord between them seemed to have abated, and, while she knew this peace wouldn't last, for some odd reason she found she liked it, and did not want to ruffle the waters.

'One way and another, I seem to be fully oc- cupied,' she murmured agreeably.

She saw Carter go still—as if some thought had just come to him. But, whatever it was, she didn't get to hear about it, because the next she knew he was saying, 'To get to my purpose in coming to see you.' Oh, no—was he going to tell her that her services were no longer re- quired after all? 'I wondered if you were busy this evening?'

Feeling little short of flabbergasted at what he had just asked, Ashlyn put her suddenly racing heart down to the tremendous surge of relief she experienced that her fears were not to be realised. Carter wanted to know if she was busy that evening? Desperately she fought for calm, and found some—he wasn't asking her for a date, for goodness' sake!

Very swiftly she did a sketchy run through of the subject-matter of their conversation so far. 'I've a feeling you're going to tell me that my small efforts for Hamilton Holdings don't end at five o'clock.'

'You're bright. But then, I've always thought so.'

She stared at him. Solemn-eyed, he stared back. Her insides went off on a pursuit of their own. 'You want something?' she guessed, and nearly fell over sideways when Carter grinned—a grin of such devastation, a grin of such unexpected charm that she was rendered speechless.

But not nearly so speechless as when, with a charm she had never suspected him of, he revealed, 'I'm entertaining a couple of business acquaintances and their wives at my place this evening,' and then asked, with a totally winning smile, 'Care to come and help?'

Carter was inviting her to his home? To dinner? To help entertain some business people? Ashlyn remembered the many beautiful women she had seen him photographed with in the Press— and he wanted *her* to help?

'Provided you don't mean with the washing-up,' she managed when she got some of her breath back. She could hardly believe it, either, when he laughed.

'I can promise you that.'

'What time?'

'Can you make a quarter to eight?'

'That should be all right,' she answered, realising he'd want her there before his guests arrived, and wanting to sprint home now and start getting ready.

'You'll need my address,' he began.

'I already know it,' she replied.

'You already know it?' He seemed mildly surprised.

'And every member of the board's address, *including telephone numbers*,' she stressed, and didn't have to say more.

'You worked late that night too,' he murmured, a smile playing about his mouth as he referred to Tuesday evening of last week when he'd made out he didn't have Joseph Fulford's home phone number and she'd had to drive over there. Plainly Carter realised that she could not have wasted any time after that in noting down all important addresses and phone numbers. 'Going to forgive me for that?' he asked, with such overwhelming charm that had she been standing she was sure her legs would have buckled.

Ashlyn did not know whether he was asking her to forgive him for the lie that he did not know Joseph Fulford's home phone number, or the fact that she'd had to break her date to deliver that message. Though, since she'd told Carter that she'd been able to keep her date anyway, it had to be his lie.

Whatever, it seemed totally unimportant just then. 'Of course,' she said on a light laugh. The moment he was gone, she rang the switchboard to say she was going home, and left her office early.

Her mother was surprised to see her home a little earlier than usual. 'I'm going out to dinner,' Ashlyn replied, aware that mystifyingly the fact that she could not tell her mother where she was going had nothing to do with the certainty that if she did all the Ainsworths would know within a very short while that she had been to dinner at Carter Hamilton's home. It just seemed private, somehow more private than business-private. Which was absurd really, because business was all it was. And, good heavens, she didn't want it to be more than that!

Thoughts of Carter seemed to dominate her mind, though, as she bathed and got ready to drive to his home. When had she ever thought him charmless? He had charm by the barrowload!

Not that he often favoured her with it, of course. But then, he hadn't ever wanted her as a member of his board. In front of everyone else he was well mannered enough to be courteous, but why would he do anything that might be construed as encouraging?

She must remember that he wanted to *dis*-courage her from being a board member. She had been in danger of forgetting, and she must not; Carter wanted her out!

Which made it all extremely confusing that, out of all the terrific-looking women he knew, it was she whom he had asked to be his hostess. A smile pulled her mouth upwards—while Carter might want her out, she could not help but feel pleased that, when it came to business, he must trust her more than he trusted any of his lady-friends.

She was on her way downstairs when it came to her that any of his lady-friends might have a previous engagement that particular night. Ashlyn cheered up when she recalled the females she had seen pictured with him, who had looked as if they hung on his every word. From what she could tell, there could never be a previous engagement that was so important that it would not be instantly broken were he to ask.

'Darling, you look wonderful!' her mother trilled.

Her mother was her biggest fan. But Ashlyn, who had butterflies in her tummy, needed to hear just then that in her simple short-sleeved, long-skirted silk dress of deep pink she looked wonderful.

'Thanks,' she mumbled, taking her car keys out of her small evening purse.

'Er—he's not someone—special, is he, darling?' Katherine Ainsworth asked gently, and Ashlyn realised that in her efforts to avoid telling her mother where and with whom she was dining she had given her food for outrageous speculation.

Carter Hamilton special! Grief! 'It's not one person in particular.' Totally unable to lie, she quickly squashed any further speculation. 'I'm dining with some business people. They...er...'

'Well, of course, if it's business!' At once her mother's expression changed. 'And it must be confidential, certainly. No—you don't have to tell me any more,' she beamed, and Ashlyn went out to her car knowing that her mother would spend the evening praying that one of her relatives might ring so that she could tell them, 'Ashlyn's out—she has a dinner engagement with some business people.'

Ashlyn found Carter's house without too much trouble. It was set in its own grounds and, as twenty minutes to eight showed on her car clock, she parked her car and went up the few steps and rang the bell.

Carter answered the door himself. 'Ashlyn.' He said her name, nothing more, and just stood there looking at her.

'Carter,' she murmured likewise. Her heart was thundering against her ribs. She had known he was good-looking but in a dinner jacket he was sensational!

'You're beautiful!' he said softly.

Her legs went like jelly. 'You're not so bad yourself,' she returned impishly—and he grinned. Oh, goodness! Was she glad of his hand on her elbow as he helped her over his threshold!

'Come and meet my housekeeper,' he invited. 'Mrs Johnson has everything under control, but it'll be as well if you have a chat with her first.'

Ashlyn hardly knew why. Mrs Johnson turned out to be a very, very efficient lady—Ashlyn could not imagine Carter hiring anyone who wasn't. 'I can see I shall be in the way if I offer to help, but feel free to give me a call in the unlikely event that you have a last-minute hitch,' Ashlyn bade her.

'Why, thank you,' Mrs Johnson smiled, and they left her to it.

Carter then showed Ashlyn the cloakroom and facilities, and, opening a door that led into his drawing room, asked, 'Would you care for something to drink?'

A stiff double of something might not be a bad idea, she felt, but since she didn't want to disgrace herself by going face down in her soup... 'A glass of tonic water would be nice,' she accepted affably—who was to know that there wasn't gin in it?

The corners of his lips moved, and she had a disconcerting idea that this clever man knew every thought that went on inside her head. He couldn't do, of course. Though when he brought her the tonic water she'd asked for, complete with the ice and lemon that most often went with a gin and tonic, she began to wonder.

'Er—is there anything I need to know—er—before your friends—guests—arrive?' she enquired in a rush. Good grief, what was the matter with her? 'Any subject you want me to avoid?'

Carter shook his head, and, coming over to the couch where she was seated, he sat down beside her. Then he smiled a reassuring kind of smile. 'Just be yourself,' he stated. At that moment she had no idea what just being herself was. Perhaps it showed, because, with his dark eyes staring down into hers, he went on, 'I've noticed, Ashlyn, that you have an intelligence and an inbuilt sensitivity that makes you a natural and sincere hostess.'

Her green eyes widened. Twice she had been in his company when he had entertained someone, both times at lunch. But... 'Me?' she questioned.

'You,' he assured her. 'And I'm not the only one to have noticed it.'

'Who...?' She used some of the intelligence he had just credited her with. 'You mean Geoff and Henry?'

Carter, as if suddenly fascinated by her dainty nose, quite unexpectedly stretched out a hand and ran a finger down it. Then the doorbell rang. Ashlyn did not know quite what startled her more—the doorbell pealing, or her skin tingling so pleasurably at his touch!

Kay and Roland Elliot and Yvonne and Fraser Griffiths were four of the nicest people she had ever met. Whatever ability Carter thought she had in the hostess department, having shaken hands with them, Ashlyn discovered that her nerves had disappeared completely, and they were soon chatting away like old friends.

The meal Mrs Johnson had prepared was delicious and unhurried, with everyone having a say in the conversation. And with everything going so splendidly Ashlyn couldn't help thinking that if she was working, then it did not feel like work. Talk just flowed about any given subject, from gardening, through music and theatre, to art.

'Yvonne paints very fine water colours,' Fraser mentioned at one point, and the conversation, which had never waned, glided on smoothly.

Ashlyn guessed that she had having so often been involved in her parents' dinner parties to thank for the fact that not once did she feel out of her depth. She even found that, as well as seeing to it that no one felt left out, if her opinion was sought she was able to contribute without allowing the subject-matter to be too contentious. And in no time, it seemed, they were on to dessert and coffee.

Then, unbelievably, the evening was over! 'You must come with Carter to a party we're having next month,' Kay Elliot invited her warmly as Ashlyn stood at the door with Carter, helping him see his guests out.

'I'd like that,' she accepted, knowing that it would not happen, but feeling strangely that she would not mind if it did.

'Goodnight, Ashlyn,' said Roland, and gave her a kiss on her cheek. She'd seen it happen a dozen times at her mother's parties—a guest saluting the hostess's cheek in parting.

'Goodnight,' she smiled—and received a kiss from Fraser Griffiths too.

She stood back as Carter closed the door after all four guests had left. She wanted to ask him how she had done and if he thought it had gone off all right, but she didn't want him to think that she was fishing. She had seen a different Carter that night. Had seen him to be considerate, courteous, witty—and a splendid host.

'Another coffee?' he suggested.

Ashlyn found she was staring up into his eyes. She felt confused. Needing to look elsewhere, she looked quickly down to her left wrist, and remembered that she wasn't wearing a watch. 'What time is it?' she asked, looking up again. There was a hint of amusement playing around his mouth, she thought.

Though his eyes seemed perfectly serious when he answered, 'Half past twelve.'

'It isn't!' she gasped. 'Truly?' Carter turned his watch round for her to see. 'Where did all those hours fly to?' she asked—they had positively sped by.

'A sure sign your hostessing was a success,' Carter replied with a smile.

Oh, Carter! What charm! That smile! 'You were the host,' she thought to remind him— and wondered if she was going light-headed. 'Er—I'd better go. Would you let Mrs Johnson know that I thought her salmon *en croute* the best I've ever tasted?'

'Certainly,' he replied, then seemed to hesitate. Looking down at her, he remarked evenly, 'It's late and you've a fair drive.' To her astonishment, he offered, 'You're welcome to one of my spare rooms if you'd prefer to drive home in the morning.'

Somehow Ashlyn managed to save her jaw from hitting the floor, so great was her surprise. His offer had been matter-of-fact, and she knew she could take it at face value. It was late, it was dark, and she was a woman. Perhaps it was the magic of the moment, but she felt that she would like to stay, perhaps get to know him a little better over another coffee before she went to bed.

'I think I'll go,' she made herself refuse. Magic of the moment! What on earth was the matter with her?

'Sorry,' Carter apologised at once with a wry look. 'I must try to treat you like one of the men.' And, with a devastating smile, he added, 'I'm still getting the hang of one of our board members being female!'

He'd noticed! She laughed. 'Chivalrous yet!' she jibed. Her heartbeat started to become erratic when laughter lit his eyes, and she turned towards the door.

Carter went with her out to her car. 'Ring me when you get home,' he instructed, and then rendered her speechless when he bent and kissed her cheek.

Ashlyn drove on automatic pilot for half an hour, barely aware of anything but the tingling sensation of Carter's lips on her cheek.

It didn't mean anything, for goodness' sake. Both Roland and Fraser had said goodnight in the same manner. So why should the feel of Carter's kiss linger?

Probably because as short a time ago as that afternoon she would have said it was inconceivable that Carter would say goodnight to her so, she decided.

She remembered so many things about him on that drive home. His courtesy to one and all. The way he had treated her as an equal. His charm. His—his—everything.

Ashlyn felt quite dreamy when she left her car and went indoors. Her parents had left lights on for her, and had gone to bed. But she knew from experience that one or the other would still be awake.

'Goodnight,' she called quietly as she passed their door.

'Goodnight, dear,' her mother answered.

Ashlyn went along to her own room. She closed the door and looked at the telephone by her bed. Carter would be asleep long since. Surely he hadn't meant it when he'd instructed her to ring him when she got home?

She collected her diary from the handbag she had used at work that day. She had his phone number. No, it was silly; she couldn't ring. He'd think she'd gone potty! Ashlyn dropped the diary down on her bed and went to her bathroom to wash and prepare for bed.

But, on returning to her bedroom, that diary seemed to haunt her. She picked it up and, placing it on her bedside table, got into bed— and knew that with Carter, Carter, Carter for some unknown reason buzzing around in her head she was just not going to sleep a wink unless she did something about it.

She picked up the diary and found his telephone number. So she'd call but if Carter didn't answer by the time it had rung five times she was going to put the phone down.

Almost as if he was sitting there with his hand on his phone, he answered straight away. She wasn't ready for him—didn't know what to say. 'Home safe,' was what she did eventually manage.

'Goodnight,' Carter murmured quietly.

Ashlyn put her receiver back on its cradle and lay down. She felt a little confused—yet she felt happy. She closed her eyes. She had a smile on her face as sleep claimed her.

CHAPTER SIX

THE weekend seemed to drag by on leaden feet. Ashlyn went out with her friends on Saturday and Sunday, as fond of them as ever. But she was ready and eager to go to work when Monday dawned. 'See you at the usual time, I expect,' she remarked to her mother on leaving.

'Unless you're delayed on some business matter,' her father chipped in.

'Bye,' she smiled, and drove to Hamilton Holdings feeling a touch anxious that both her parents seemed to have blown up her role out of all proportion. Though, on thinking about it, she didn't suppose many of the chairman's staff were invited into his home to act as hostess. But her parents didn't know about that!

Ashlyn entered her office wondering what the day would bring. Would Carter perhaps pop in to say hello? She felt that they were on better terms now than they had been.

She heard the lift stop many times and each time masculine footsteps neared her door she felt flustered. Then she wondered—as those footsteps went straight on past and faded away—what she was getting flustered about.

The only person she saw in that first hour was Ivy. 'Are you all right for tea and coffee?' she wanted to know.

'Fine, thanks, Ivy. Have you time for a cup?'

'Why not?' Ivy answered, looking decidedly wicked. 'They'll never think of looking for me here!'

Ashlyn laughed—and was laughing again later when Vezio Morini telephoned her from Italy. They fell to speaking in Italian straight away. She soon discovered that his call was not a business call; Vezio told her that he had thought of nothing but her since meeting her last Thursday. She had to smile.

'It's very kind of you to say so,' she replied. If nothing else, Vezio was extremely good for the ego.

'It's true!' he protested, sounding upset that she might not believe him. He was still going on at length when her office door opened— and Carter stood there. She felt her cheeks go pink and, as Carter came in and sat himself down, she wished that Vezio—who was just coming to the point of his call—would hang up. 'Which is why, since my schedule has me tied up here for the next week, I ask if you would like to fly here for dinner tonight. I can arrange a plane for you,' he stated, making her blink.

Realising some comment from her was required, Ashlyn, not looking at Carter but aware that he was waiting his patient best for her to end her call, told Vezio that she didn't think so. She caught a movement from Carter when he heard her speaking Italian and was certain he knew to whom she was talking. She confirmed it when, thanking her caller nicely, she ended, *'Arrivederci*, Vezio.' Ashlyn's heart was drumming wildly when she put down the phone. She glanced at Carter—and her spirits promptly nose-dived. Gone was the charm of Friday. Grim-faced, he stared at her. Ashlyn did not bother to ask why he had come to see her—she guessed she would have it fired at her, both barrels, soon enough.

'I didn't know Morini was in London!' Carter barked—clearly put out about something.

Well, she didn't have to take that from anybody. 'He isn't!' she snapped. Goodness, she wanted her head looking at! She had been happy after spending an evening in his company! How crass could you get? 'Vezio phoned from Italy.'

'To speak to me?'

It was a legitimate question—she was, after all, there to take calls from people like Vezio when Carter wasn't around. Carter didn't have his briefcase with him, but that didn't mean he hadn't only just arrived for the day.

'No. To speak to me,' she replied.

That didn't appear to please Carter either. 'What about?' he snarled.

Damn him! 'It was personal!' she flared.

'He's never met you!'

That stopped her in her tracks. Quite obviously it hadn't been Carter who had told Vezio where to find her last Thursday, as she had thought. 'Correction—I met him last week.' Sort that! she fumed.

He did! 'He came here looking for you?' Ashlyn stubbornly refused to answer—but that didn't sweeten Carter any. 'And on the strength of one meeting he's making personal calls to you?' he challenged.

Dammit, he made it sound as if she had a face like the back of a bus. This was no time for false modesty! 'It happens!' she erupted, sparks flashing in her eyes. Double dammit!

'All the time!' she added for good measure. Who did he think he was?

'I don't doubt it,' Carter grated, now on his feet and looking ready to throttle her.

Good—she loved him too. 'In this case, Vezio invited me to dine with him in Italy tonight.' She was nowhere near to backing down. 'Should I go, do you think?' she asked, and had her breath catch the back of her throat at his answer.

'Not if you want to come back a virgin!' he snarled. With that, he was on his way out.

Ashlyn was so outraged at what he had just said that if she'd had a hatchet handy she'd have thrown it at his back. How dared he? How *dared* he say that to her?

She was too angry to stay seated. Too angry to stay where she was. Too angry to lift her phone to tell the switchboard where she was going. Ashlyn went and took herself off for a walk.

Diabolical swine! When had she ever thought that she and Carter were on better terms now than they had been? Just let him ask her to be his hostess a second time. Just let him! Hanging, drawing and quartering were too good for the vitriolic tyke!

It was half past eleven when Ashlyn returned to her office. She had been in two minds about returning at all. Then she'd remembered her parents, and their pride. Add to that how extremely upset and disappointed they would be even though they knew that the job was only temporary and to return to Hamilton Holdings seemed to be the better, if unpalatable, option.

She had been back barely a minute when her phone rang. Her fight was with Carter, not the company. Ashlyn donned her professional hat and picked up the phone.

'Feeling better?'

It was *him*! His gall! She had never felt ill! 'It must have been something disagreeable I came across,' she replied, somehow managing to make her voice as cool as his.

'Well, now that it's out of your system...' Was he asking for it! 'The thing is, aware as I am of your many talents...'

Was he being funny? She gave him the benefit of the doubt, though why, when she knew what an out-and-out monster he could be, she couldn't have said. 'What do you mean exactly?' she asked, ready to slam down the phone at the first word of insult.

'Excellent hostess, trilingual—' he began to enumerate—and Ashlyn could feel her crossness ebbing.

'So I speak a few languages,' she interrupted, inexplicably discovering a need to keep her feet firmly on the ground.

'More than three?' Carter enquired.

She had no idea where this conversation was leading. But it was fairly evident, for all his voice had lost its cool edge and was starting to sound quite pleasant, that he had not rung her to apologise for his earlier remarks.

'Well—yes,' she answered.

'French?'

Ah. Light began to dawn—obviously he had some French guest he was entertaining to lunch and wanted her assistance. A feeling of excitement started to pulse through her veins and in an instant Ashlyn had forgotten every bit about not helping him entertain ever again.

'Of course,' she replied confidently. French was one of her best languages.

There was a pause at the other end, and she waited, ready to make a note of what time and where they would be eating. Therefore she was positively thunderstruck when Carter finally drawled, 'Now isn't that fortunate? I have to go to Paris this afternoon—you can come with me.'

'Par— Me! B-but...' Utterly stunned, she could barely take it in.

'You have a problem with that?' Carter asked curtly, and Ashlyn realised that, playing in a business field, she was acting less than professionally.

'None at all!' she answered equally curtly. 'Just tell me what time, and for how long—and should I bring the family pearls?'

She thought she heard him smother a laugh, but knew she was mistaken when, still in the same curt tone, he stated, 'I'll see you at the airport at four-thirty. I'm not sure how long we'll be there.' He waited only to tell her, 'You'd better cancel all your social engagements for this week.' Then he put down his phone.

Ashlyn still didn't know whether to believe it or not. Her phone still in her hand, she starred at the instrument. She was going to France—with Carter! All too plainly that was why he had called by earlier—to tell her about it in person. Only she had annoyed him with her prattle about should she go to Italy that night—on a personal matter—when he had plans for her to go to France on a business matter.

If only he'd said. Pride was the very devil, she realised. Quite clearly, when he'd asked her whether she spoke French, Carter had been saying that he could not. And, not wishing to own up to it, he and his pride had taken refuge in slamming into her.

Oh, Carter. As if it mattered that he could not speak French. Dear Carter... Suddenly Ashlyn felt tremendously alive. As if anything mattered! She was in love with him, loved him, loved him, loved him—and she was going to France with him.

Her next reaction was to feel overwhelmingly dazed. She *loved* him? She slowly put down the phone. She loved him? Was in love with him? She shook her head as if to deny it. But it was a fact! She had been in love with him last Friday, and that explained why she had gone to bed so happy. She had been in love with him and hadn't known it—most probably, now she came to think of it, she had been in love with him before then.

Fifteen minutes later Ashlyn was still sitting coming to terms with her startling and un-looked-for discovery. It was just then that she realised that to race home, pack, get ready *and* be at the airport for four-thirty was impossible.

She did what any girl would do in the circumstances. She rang her mother. 'You've only just caught me—I was on my way out!' Katherine Ainsworth commented.

'Were you going anywhere special?' Ashlyn asked fearfully.

'No—just taking a look at the shops.'

'You couldn't do me a ginormous favour, could you?' Ashlyn asked.

'I'll try. What is it?'

Ashlyn could see no way of hiding that she might not be home for a week, nor where she was going, particularly since she was enlisting her mother's help.

'The thing is, it's just been dropped on me that I'm flying to France later today—and I just can't—'

'You're going to France!' her mother exclaimed. 'On business?' she questioned, and was nearly ecstatic when she heard who with. Then, efficiency being her middle name, she shared Ashlyn's problem and was soon making light of it.

Ashlyn replaced her phone knowing that at around two-thirty, or before, traffic permitting, her mother would arrive with her passport and a suitcase packed with everything she would need for the next few days. If that swine Carter, that dear swine Carter, thought he had given her something of a stiff initiative test, then, thanks to her mother, she would come through with flying colours.

Geoff stopped by and she gave him a cup of coffee. 'Lunch with me tomorrow?' he asked.

'Sorry,' she smiled. 'Prior engagement.' Last Friday she would have told him that she was going to Paris, but today she found that she could not. For all it was business, it somehow came under that 'private' heading, as it had on Friday evening when she had been unable to tell her mother and father where she was going.

'I can see I'll have to book lunch with you weeks in advance at this rate,' he grumbled, but smiled, as he usually did.

At one o'clock her phone rang. It was Carter, and her heart jumped, then plummeted. Was he ringing to tell her the French trip was off?

He wasn't, apparently, but his tone was back to being curt—Lord knew why she loved the brute. 'I thought you'd have left to throw a few things in a case ages ago!' he said.

Throw a few things in a case—for Paris? The man had no idea! 'Oh, I can buy anything I haven't got with me when I get there,' she floated back at him airily. 'Though, while you're on the line, it might be an idea if I know which airport to drive to.'

Carter told her, then questioned, 'You're going straight from the office?'

'I thought I would.'

'I'll drive you in my car.'

Lovely thought! But Ashlyn counselled herself to be steady. 'I'll need my car to drive home when we get back,' she stated. Carter hadn't said when that would be. Hamilton Holdings might have closed down for the day, her car shut up in a locked car park, for all she knew.

He put down the phone. Spleenish toad! she thought crossly. But because she loved him she was able to laugh. He might be the one in charge now, but she was the one who was going to translate French into English.

At two o'clock she went down to Reception to wait for her mother. Katherine Ainsworth—a thrilled Katherine Ainsworth, it had to be said—arrived at ten past two, wheeling a very large suitcase. She was also carrying a plastic suit carrier.

'You're a gem.' Ashlyn gave her mother a kiss as she relieved her of the suitcase. 'Would you like to come up and see where I work?'

'Would I ever!' On the way up in the lift her mother explained the plastic carrier. 'I thought I remembered you wearing that grey suit this morning. Really not good enough for Paris,' her smart mother went on. 'So I brought that green two-piece that suits you so well.'

'Did I say you were a gem?' Ashlyn smiled, and once they were in her office she changed into the green two-piece while her mother made a cup of coffee.

'That's much better. Now here's your passport. Your father's over the moon about how well you're getting on.'

'It is only temporary.' Ashlyn thought she should mention it, hating the thought more than her mother. Dear heaven, Ashlyn felt desolate at just the thought of never seeing Carter again. But she had this time with him in Paris to look forward to, and she wasn't going to think of anything so awful as what would happen when Lorna Stokes returned and everything was back to normal in his office again.

'Now, I'm not going to hold you up, but I insist on knowing all the non-confidential bits and pieces when you come home,' Katherine Ainsworth stated once she had finished her coffee. And Ashlyn, remembering how confusing she had found the corridors until she had got used to who worked where, went down in the lift with her mother to see her off.

She went down in the lift again with her suitcase a little while later. No way was she going to leave it until the last minute to get to the airport. Carter would just love that, wouldn't he? Plane ready to take off and no French-speaking Director of Senior Communications!

That thought made her laugh, and she wondered if being in love had made her feather-headed. But, feather-headed or not, she arrived at the airport in good time, and was there, ready and waiting, when Carter, suitcase and briefcase in his hands, strode in.

He spotted her straight away, though whether because of where she had positioned herself or because he was the sort of man who missed nothing she was hard put to tell.

Carter halted by her, his dark gaze raking over her smart two-piece, and she realised that, unbelievably, he remembered she had been wearing something different that morning. His glance then went down to the large case by her side, and she could just feel a laugh bubbling up inside her.

'A girl's best friend is her mother,' she murmured, and just loved it when, after a moment of staring down at her in stony silence, suddenly he laughed too.

He was serious, though, when a moment later he transferred his glance to her suitcase. 'Can you manage that?' he enquired.

With him beside her, in laughing mood, she could have managed ten of them. 'No problem,' she assured him, and, tucking his briefcase under the arm that held his suitcase, he took her by the elbow with the other and guided her, as she wheeled her own luggage, in the direction of the check-in desk.

They seemed to be airborne before she knew it, and she half expected Carter to take out some work and get on with it. But, to her pleasant surprise, he seemed content to relax and to while away the hour in either desultory conversation or a sort of companionable silence.

There were questions she would have liked to ask. Questions about what sort of business they were going to be doing in Paris. But, with Carter seeming disinclined to talk business, and realising how hard he worked, Ashlyn felt that to let him relax while he could might be a much better idea.

She felt relaxed too, she had to own, though she began to feel a little tense when Carter thought to refer to the fact that her mother must have packed her a case and delivered it to the office, asking, 'Your parents don't mind you flying off at short notice?'

'It's not something I do every day,' she answered, realising that they were getting close to the way she had intimated she might fly that evening to Italy and have dinner with Vezio. She just couldn't bear to have another spat with Carter. Which left her, in her efforts to take the conversation away from anything that might cause an upset, diving into another area which she did not particularly want to discuss either. But she stated quite openly, 'To be honest, my parents are enormously pleased that—' She broke off.

'Don't leave it there,' Carter encouraged, and added, with a smile that caused her heart to tilt, 'I have every admiration for honesty.'

She guessed that in business honesty was his watchword. And, encouraged by him to go on, she found herself telling him, 'Well, to start at the beginning, my father decided way back that he didn't want to go into the family business, Ainsworth Engineering. So, with some financial help from my grandfather, he set up Ainsworth Cables.' A week ago she'd have told him none of this. But a week ago she hadn't known that she was in love with him. And now, especially when he was so encouraging, she didn't seem able to stop talking. 'Anyhow, it soon became a matter of enormous pride to him that as Ainsworth Engineering went from strength to strength Ainsworth Cables did too. He worked so hard, but...' She faltered.

'But hard wasn't good enough when his plans and investments went awry,' Carter took up quietly. It was plain to her then that he knew far more about her father's business than she did.

So she agreed, and added, 'And you came along and bought him out.'

'Does that bother you?' Carter asked, turning so he could see her face.

She shook her head. 'I think now that it's the best thing that could have happened to him. He's not looking anywhere near as worn as he once did. Though...' she hesitated.

'Though?' Carter prompted.

'Well, the thing is...' Ashlyn felt compelled to go on '...my father's pride was very badly dented because he had to let the firm go.' Suddenly she realised that they were sailing close to another dangerous area—that of her father holding out for a seat on the board for her—and she hurried on, 'So he—er—needed something else he could be proud of to his brothers and their families.'

'He found it in you,' Carter stated intuitively.

'I'm afraid so,' she acknowledged, and, since Carter appreciated honesty so much, she found herself confessing, 'He's told them that I'm now an executive director with Hamilton Holdings.' She looked into his dark grey eyes. He didn't seem to have taken exception to the title her father had pinned on her. 'It's his pride, you see,' she ended quietly.

She was totally charmed when, with a gentle smile for her, he commented, 'You've a whole lot of pride too, Ashlyn Ainsworth.'

She turned to look out of the window, her heart racing. She could not remember just then why or how it had come about that Carter had witnessed her pride. But she felt a warm glow at what had sounded like a compliment. That glow stayed with her long after their plane had landed.

They went by taxi from the airport and Ashlyn realised that Carter must have stayed at the same hotel before, because he was able to tell the driver where to take them. When they arrived at a large and well-lit building, she guessed Carter must have read the fare on the meter, for, as he paid the driver and received a cordial, *'Merci beaucoup, monsieur,'* at the size of his tip, he had no need of her French-speaking services.

He had a smattering of French, she observed; he was able to briefly greet the concierge on duty. But there her observations ended because, all at once, it came to her that this was not a hotel but an apartment block!

Startled, she looked to Carter, but he and the concierge were busy holding open the lift doors and manhandling their two cases inside.

Trying to keep her mind a blank—she didn't know how she was going to feel if she was to share an apartment with him—she stepped into the lift and she and Carter sailed upwards.

She loved him and the idea of being constantly in his company was little short of wonderful. But, because of her love for him, and because of that pride he had spoken of, it was of the utmost importance that Carter, with his quick mind and eyes, did not see in such close and continued confines so much as a glimpse of her love.

By the time they had stepped out of the lift and he had unlocked the door of his apartment, Ashlyn was feeling on very shaky ground. She'd just die if he knew how she felt about him.

'It's an apartment!' she stated flatly as they went in.

'You're quick—I'll give you that!' he mocked, and Ashlyn was glad of his mockery; it annoyed her, and she needed to be annoyed.

'I'm to sleep here?' she questioned tautly, and saw his good humour abruptly vanish.

'If it's not too much trouble,' he answered shortly.

'But—' she went to object.

'Forgive me,' he cut in, not looking sorry at all. 'This apartment belongs to the company and it's where we on the board make our base when we're here on company business.' His dark eyes bored into her, and she felt like a worm on the end of a pin. 'Forgive me,' he apologised again, 'for looking on you merely as another board member.'

Ashlyn turned from him, feeling about as big as tuppence. She'd had a dressing down, and she guessed she deserved it. But—and oh, what a contradictory creature love had made of her—she didn't want him to see her 'merely as another board member'. Mixed-up she might be in worrying about sharing an apartment with him, but she didn't want him to see her as one of the men; she wanted him to see her as a woman.

'Which room are you having?' she questioned snappily, looking around the stylishly furnished sitting room at the many doors leading off.

'The best one, naturally!' he returned without pause, and she just had to laugh. His mouth twitched when he saw that she was over her cross-patch moment, and as quickly as it had come all enmity was over. 'I'll take your case in,' he commented. Ashlyn hung back.

She watched as he picked up her case and noted to which room he took it, as well as noticing his chivalry—he hadn't left it to her to struggle with it over the thickly piled carpet.

She needed a moment by herself, she realised. They were friends again—well, of a sort, she qualified. But she still felt a little tense somehow, and instinctively wandered in the opposite direction. She was in the kitchen when she heard Carter come and join her.

'Someone's stocked up the fridge,' she remarked off the top of her head.

'As per instructions,' he replied easily.

'I'd better go and unpack,' she returned. Carter seemed taller, more dominant than ever in the close confines of the kitchen.

'You'd better take this with you,' he stayed her, and gave her a bulky envelope.

'What is it?' she asked, innocently expecting it to be instructions or an itinerary for the next few days.

'Local currency,' he answered, and she was immediately up in arms.

'I don't want it!' she exclaimed furiously, pushing it back at him.

'Oh, for G——' He broke off, exasperated. 'Stow your pride for a minute and be realistic!' he rapped. 'You're in France and you'll need——'

'I can get my own currency tomorrow. From a bank—anywhere.'

'You don't have to. I——'

'I don't want your money,' she insisted.

'Then look on it as business expenses,' he thundered. 'I collected it for you from Finance on my way out. If you really insist, I'll instruct them when we get back to deduct what you've spent out of your salary cheque. Now go and——'

'Salary cheque?' she queried.

And as suddenly as the storm had blown in it was again over. 'I just don't believe there's a woman like you!' Carter declared, tilting his head and studying her. 'Had you no idea that a salary cheque was paid into your bank account at the end of last month?'

Witlessly she stared at him. 'Honestly?' she exclaimed. 'What for?' she asked, only for her world to spin crazily when Carter, after a split second of just looking at her, stretched out his hands to her arms.

And, as if he couldn't prevent himself, he pulled her a little closer. 'For doing what you do so brilliantly,' he smiled, and dropped a gossamer-light kiss upon her cheek. Then, swiftly, he pushed her away. 'Now go and get ready; we're dining with friends of mine in an hour.'

Ashlyn felt too choked to argue. She went quickly, glad that her bedroom had its own bathroom. She needed to shower and to change and she was such a dither inside she didn't know when she would ever be ready to see Carter again.

Striving hard to be practical—Carter had kissed her, be it only on her cheek, be it a kiss that meant precisely nothing—she went to unpack her suitcase.

Her mother had gone a little demented, she saw: not only had she packed the clothes Ashlyn had said she thought might be suitable, but she had also packed two dresses which she had not mentioned. One was plain black, finished just above the knee and was classic; the other, which Ashlyn just couldn't see herself wearing this trip, was a narrow-strapped, fitted dress of deep gold. With it came a matching stole.

Carter had said that they were dining with friends of his in an hour—she'd better get a move on.

Her thoughts as she got ready centred mainly on Carter. She realised that she had better stop taking exception to the least little thing he said, if she didn't want him to think her tiresome. Or, worse, supposing he started looking beneath the surface for a reason? Not that the bundle of French francs he'd given her came under the heading of 'least little thing', she mused. She started to smile as she recalled Carter's flattering 'doing what you do so brilliantly'. Fancy—and she got paid for it! She vaguely recalled someone from Finance wanting details of her bank account but she had thought that was so they could bank her cheque for attending the board meeting direct.

By the time she had her hair neatly dressed in its usual thick coil at the back of her head, Ashlyn was beginning to feel apprehensive again. She had opted to wear the black dress her mother had thought to put in, and she knew that she was looking good. But nerves were playing havoc with her insides.

Knowing that if she didn't go soon Carter would come knocking at her door, wanting to know what the hold-up was, she picked up her dainty black evening purse, straightened her shoulders, and opened her bedroom door.

'Good, you're re—' Carter broke off, his eyes going over her from the tip of her head, skimming her shape, and on down to her toes. 'Did anybody ever tell you you've got the most sensational legs?' he enquired, his eyes on her warm green ones.

'Er—' Her heart was drumming like blazes; she couldn't handle it. 'You don't have to take me with you!' she said in a rush.

'Just because I said you've got good legs?' he teased.

And she loved him. Oh, how she loved him. 'You said you were dining with friends,' she reminded him. If they were friends of his, then they would speak English, which made her role as interpreter redundant. 'I can knock something together out of the fridge.'

'Not in that get-up, you can't.' He smiled a gentle smile, and she loved him some more. Then he was all bracing and matter-of-fact. 'Come on, woman,' he said, his tone brooking no argument, 'I'm starving, and the concierge has a taxi waiting.'

Solène Ducret was an elegant woman of about thirty. Luc, her charming husband, was the same age as Carter. The friends greeted each other warmly and when Carter introduced her Ashlyn was made to feel most welcome.

She took to the French couple straight away, and, as she had surmised they would, everyone spoke in English. Ashlyn felt all the signs were good for an excellent evening.

Indeed, things were going along splendidly, everyone relaxed and at ease as they moved to their table in the restaurant. Ashlyn had thought her services might be required to translate the menu for Carter, but an English translation was already given, so she concentrated on her own selection.

'Do you have a career as well as your board duties, Ashlyn?' Solène enquired as their first course arrived.

'I'm—working temporarily full-time for the company.' Ashlyn had hesitated over the word 'working'. It did not seem at all like work.

'Ashlyn's an executive in her own right,' Carter put in, and Ashlyn felt slightly jolted. Was he being funny—or was he being serious? Having only that day discovered she loved him, she was so highly sensitive to anything he said or did that her judgement had become unsure.

'And enjoying it,' she smiled, and thought it time to take the conversation elsewhere. 'Do you follow a career, Solène?' she enquired, and heard that Solène was a scientist.

Ashlyn thought Solène's career most interesting and, while being careful to give the others space, formed a queue of questions to ask. The evening progressed so easily that it was time to leave almost before Ashlyn knew it.

'Are you in Paris for long?' Solène asked as they stood on the pavement saying goodnight. 'Perhaps we could meet again...'

'We're here until the end of the week,' Carter answered for Ashlyn, and Ashlyn's feeling of well-being surged. They were there, she and Carter, for a whole week! Well, nearly a whole week! Oh, joy, oh, bliss.

Carter was saying something about how he would arrange something with Luc, then they said their goodnights and turned to get into the waiting taxi. Ashlyn felt as if she was dreaming and she never wanted to wake up.

But she did wake up—with a very big bump. For Luc had stepped forward hurriedly and, in the urgency of the moment, forgot to speak

English. 'Carter—*où nous retrouverons-nous demain*?'

'*Je viendrai vous prendre à votre hôtel à huit heures,*' Carter answered.

The taxi pulled away from the kerb and Ashlyn settled back. Carter and Luc obviously had some business to do first thing in the morning. Carter had told him that he'd pick him up at his hotel at eight. Suddenly, she froze!

In slow motion she played back Luc's 'Carter—where shall we meet tomorrow?' and Carter's 'I'll pick you up at your hotel at eight'. Carter had replied in perfect French, with not a falter, not a stumble! Not only had he instantly understood Luc's question but, without having to think about it, he had replied in the same tongue! Carter was as fluent in French as she was!

So where did that leave her? What in blue blazes was she doing there, since it was blatantly obvious that Carter needed neither interpreter nor translator?

'Is something the matter, Ashlyn?'

You could say that! He was quick—she'd give him that. He must have picked up, either from the stiff way she was sitting or from some other means, the fact that her happy mood of a few minutes ago had changed. Well, bubbles to him—she needed to think.

'No!' she answered shortly, and did not thank him that he chose not to pursue the matter.

Swine! She tried hard to remember what he had said when he had roped her into going to Paris with him, but she just could not remember. Not word for word anyhow, because seconds later she had realised that she was in love with him—and nothing after that had made sense in her head for a little while.

Well, it was for sure he didn't need her for her languages, and it was for sure that since they had been entertained that evening he didn't need her there to help him and . . . Oh, heavens, Solène and Luc were sophisticated people. What in creation were they thinking? Carter had introduced her as a member of his board—but did they really believe that?

Her face flamed scarlet. Surely they didn't believe . . . ? Carter would never . . . Well, he had kissed her cheek earlier that evening, but it hadn't meant anything. She might still be a little wet behind the ears about that sort of thing but she just knew that Carter wasn't like that. That his kiss meant nothing.

And she hated him for that too. Because she loved him, felt mixed-up and confused. And he was clever, and she knew he must have some motive in bringing her to Paris with him, but she'd be darned if she could fathom out what it—

'Do you want to go around again?'

Carter's curt tones cut into her thoughts, and made her aware that the taxi had stopped and that he had got out and was waiting for her to join him—they had arrived back at the apartment.

Without a word she got out of the taxi, and, her chin tilted a proud fraction, without a word she preceded him into the building. Mute, she walked into the lift. She felt humiliated and embarrassed that because he must feel responsible for her he hadn't been able to leave her behind in the apartment. She loved him and hated the fact that he must have felt obliged to take her with him. How could he? As the lift sailed upwards, she felt like hitting him.

The lift stopped and she walked in front to the door of the apartment. Stiff-backed, wooden-expressioned, she wouldn't look at him. He opened the door; she marched in. Indeed, she was halfway across the sitting-room floor when a hand clamped over her wrist and stopped her.

He stopped her and turned her, and Ashlyn came the closest she had come yet to hitting him. 'Let go of me!' she ordered angrily.

As she might have expected, he ignored her order. 'So what did I do?' he demanded. There was a look of determination to get to the bottom of this on his face.

'You *know* what you did!' she erupted.

'I took you to dine with some friends. Up until fifteen minutes ago I'd have said you enjoyed it,' he answered toughly.

'It's never pleasant to be taken for a fool!' she spat.

'Who took you for a fool?'

'Let go of my wrist!'

'Answer me!' Carter insisted sharply.

'You understand and speak French fluently!' she charged.

'When did I say that I couldn't?' he countercharged.

That stopped her dead. Oh, how she wished that she could remember. 'You intimated—' She broke off when his right eyebrow rose a fraction. 'Well, you led me to believe...'

'I did nothing of the kind!' he retorted. 'If your imagination has taken over, there's nothing I can do about it. My memory of our conversation is that I asked you if you could speak French, you said you could, and I asked you to come to Paris with me.'

Given that her memory of the conversation was hazy, she was positive there had been no asking about it. The arrogant swine had ordered her to go with him.

'Why?' she asked bluntly. 'Since I've heard for myself that you can speak the language every bit as well as me, why? Why me?' That had him, she was sure of it! He certainly looked at her askance—as if surprised she should take issue over it.

'You've one hell of a nerve, Miss Ainsworth,' he told her coolly, his dark eyes fixed on her. 'But, given that I'm unused to explaining myself to anyone...' oh, grief, she was in for another put-down, she could tell! '...permit me to tell you that, your fluency in the French language apart, I needed a board member with me on this trip. And you, believe it or not,' he added silkily, 'are the only member of the board who isn't up to his ears in work.'

One of these days she was going to take the greatest delight in boxing *his ears*, and it had nothing to do with the fact that he was treating her like one of the men again.

'Nice to know I have my uses!' she flared. 'So why take me with you tonight? That wasn't business.'

'You'd deny me the pleasure of dining with friends?'

'No—but...' Those dark eyes didn't seem so cold now. They were disconcerting, off-putting, 'But you didn't have to take me with you,' she managed to finish.

'Would you have my friend Luc have the opinion that only French women are beautiful?' Carter charmed the heart out of her.

Was he saying that he thought her beautiful? It was almost enough to go to bed on. 'You're—er—um—still holding...' Her voice was suddenly too husky to be heard. Ashlyn gave a small cough, and her voice was a little stronger when she asked, 'C-can I have my wrist back, please?'

'Of course,' he murmured, but instead of letting go he brought her hand up, bent his head, and kissed the back of it. Her legs went like jelly. 'Forgive me?' he asked softly, his look suddenly warm.

'Of course,' she borrowed his words, too far gone now to remember what, if anything, she had to forgive him for. But, just to show she really did forgive, she somehow felt compelled to stretch up on tiptoe and, as he had to her earlier that evening, lean forward and kiss his cheek. Immediately her lips came into contact with his skin, however, she drew back. 'I'm sorry...' her colour flared '...I shouldn't have d—'

'Oh, but I'm glad you did,' he smiled, and, purely to make her feel better about what she had done, she was sure, he bent down, and lightly placed his mouth over her own.

It was meant to be a light kiss, Ashlyn knew that, and she was sure that Carter knew that as well. But, having made a minuscule movement towards him, she felt too paralysed to move away. His mouth, his sensational mouth, was over hers, and it was wonderful.

Her hands went to his waist, perhaps to steady herself—she was never afterwards sure. But she guessed that Carter must have read her action as encouragement, for he did not back away, but gently took her in his arms. That light kiss gave way to a warm embrace.

It was sheer and perfect heaven to be in his arms. Ashlyn wrapped herself around him and held on tightly. The pressure of his lips against hers increased, and she was learning, being teased, her mouth tormented.

Somehow, hardly aware that either of them had moved, she felt his body hard up against her own, and felt an insane desire to be closer still to him. It had never happened before.

Carter kissed her again, and the fire that had begun in her started to burn brightly. She kissed him back, instinctively moulding her body against his.

She heard a sound leave him. Did he desire her? She knew she was going out of control. Yet she loved him, loved him. Did it matter?

Their lips met again; she wanted more. She felt his wonderful sensitive fingers in her hair. Suddenly felt her long, red-gold tresses fall about her shoulders as Carter released them from their pins.

'Even more beautiful than I imagined,' he breathed, standing back, looking at her. And a moment later he was burying his head in the clouds of her sweet-smelling hair.

Then he was kissing her again, the tempo of his kisses suddenly changing. The next time he moulded her to him, she knew that she was losing all sense of reality. Losing all sense...

But she did not care. And yet... Quickly, while she still could, she jerked back, her breath catching in her throat. 'You're nervous?' he asked, his tone gentle, not demanding.

She swallowed, but told him honestly, 'I like kissing you. Only...' She faltered, almost told him about this fire of awareness that had flickered into life in her and was now starting to scorch her. This dangerous fire of awareness that made it a nonsense for her to be jerking away when she wanted to be closer, even closer...

'Only?' he teased, planting the tenderest of kisses on one corner of her mouth.

'Only I think I'm getting a little out of my depth,' she answered, and stretched up to kiss a corner of *his* mouth. She wanted, wanted oh, so badly, to move her mouth along until their lips met again. But from somewhere she found the strength to pull all the way out of his arms. 'And,' she said on a gulp of breath, and with the lightest laugh she could manage, aware that she wanted him, aware that Carter desired her, 'I'm not sure that I want to do more than paddle in the shallows.'

With that, she left him. She went to her room. She went quickly. Went before she gave in to her love, and her need to be held, caressed and made love to by the man she loved.

CHAPTER SEVEN

IT TOOK Ashlyn an age to get to sleep that night.
Half of her was still regretting that she had
pulled back from Carter the way she had, while
the other half was certain that she had done the
right thing.

Would Carter have made her his, though?
Things had been heading that way, and it hadn't
been him who had backed away, had it? Uncertain if she had been right to come to her
room when she had, Ashlyn knew it would be
wonderful to be made love to by Carter. But
what happened then? Where did one go from
there? Back to London—and forget it?

She remembered the lovely and, yes, worldly
women she had seen him photographed with.
They would accept that. They knew the rules.
But she—she did not. And, had they lain
together, the thought of going back to the way
they had been once they were back in London
was one she doubted she could have coped with.

Ashlyn got up early next morning, realising
that, on balance, perhaps it was better that she

had not been any more intimate with Carter. But once she was showered, dressed, and with her hair fixed in a neat chignon, she went into the sitting room, and a mixture of emotions took her, so that a tide of pink warmed her skin.

Carter was there, up, dressed, reading a French newspaper. 'Good morning,' she offered as he got to his feet. She had been kissed by that wonderful mouth, had kissed back, clung to him pressed close to him ...

Like a douche of cold water, his cool 'Good morning' told her that he had already filed what had been momentous for her under 'pleasant while it lasted' and placed it in the 'dead' drawer. He checked his watch; a minute ago hers had said seven-fifteen. 'Your presence isn't strictly necessary at this morning's negotiations. If you want to shop...' With that sentence, he put her firmly in her place.

'Oh, good,' she beamed, tilting her chin upwards, hating him, hating him. How dared he treat her like some feather-brained shopaholic? He went over and picked up his briefcase—he didn't have to be at Luc's hotel until eight! She knew that for a fact. 'See you later, then,' she said offhandedly, already heading for the kitchen. She had a feeling she was going to howl and no dastardly male had the right to make a woman feel that way.

Carter's voice, however, stopped her mid-flight. 'You'll definitely be needed at lunch,' he stated. She halted, refusing to turn, refusing to look at him, and he went on to tell her where to meet him and at what time.

'I'll be there,' she confirmed, hating him some more because he didn't want her with him that morning, but considered her all right to have lunch with. 'Hope your negotiations go well,' she offered, and went on kitchenwards.

She was still in the kitchen when she heard the outer door close. But she no longer felt like crying. She felt angry. So she'd kissed him—but he'd kissed her first! To the devil with him!

She took a cup of coffee with her back to the sitting room and, taking a seat by a small table, saw that Carter had left her what must be a key to the apartment. Nice of him to tell her about it. What was he afraid of—that he'd get contaminated if their hands accidentally touched as he passed the key over? Oh, Carter, she sighed—and her anger was gone.

Ashlyn had not the slightest intention of going shopping. Then, at eight-fifteen, the phone rang. Her heart somersaulted; she was convinced that it was Carter. He had reached Luc's hotel and had remembered something.

She strove hard for a cool note when she picked up the phone and said, 'Hello,' but her voice was impervious to her brain's instructions.

But, in any case, it was not Carter who was on the phone, though the call did come from Luc's hotel. It was Luc's wife, Solène. Ashlyn had learned last night that Solène was having a few days' holiday from her work to be in Paris with her husband. 'Carter has just said that you are going shopping. I so seldom get to Paris,' Solène revealed, 'I wonder if I may come with you?'

'I'd love your company!' Ashlyn exclaimed, adaptable and not seeing why she should stay moping in the apartment because of *him*. Love was making a nonsense of her.

Solène was a charming companion and knew exactly where to shop. Ashlyn spotted a suit that screamed out 'Take me home', and could not resist it.

By eleven-fifteen they had both purchased a suit. Ashlyn knew by then that Solène would be at lunch with them too, and that it would be quite a big affair.

'Shall we wear our new clothes?' Solène suggested.

'Why not?' Ashlyn fell in with her. 'I'll need to go back to the apartment...'

'And I'll need to go back to my hotel...'

Simultaneously they hailed taxis, and parted. Ashlyn was aware that Carter would expect her on the dot of twelve-thirty and knew that she had not a moment to lose.

At twelve twenty-eight precisely, another taxi dropped an immaculately turned out red-headed woman outside a Paris hotel. She wore a light pure wool suit of pastel green. The straight skirt came to just above her comely knees. The jacket had short sleeves and a high stand-up collar which stood away from her neck and showed off the slender, elegant white column of her throat to perfection.

Ashlyn went towards the hotel doors, the thought of seeing Carter causing her insides to churn and making her entirely unaware of the admiring looks she was receiving. A smartly uniformed doorman held the door open for her at once.

She thanked him kindly. Going through the lobby, she searched about for the room where the private lunch party was being held. She found it and went and stood at the entrance, but could not see Carter.

'If I said before that you're beautiful, it was an understatement,' a voice she would know anywhere commented into her left ear.

'Carter!' She turned, smiling, all her earlier enmity forgotten.

'You look stunning,' he stated softly, and she knew that if he kept this up she was going to melt.

'You know that salary you spoke of?' she queried, desperately trying to remind herself that Carter's manners were such that he wouldn't make her look small in public, and that she mustn't get carried away by his compliments. 'Well, I think I'm going to need it. I—er—bought this suit this morning.'

He smiled, and her legs went like water. He looked into her eyes, and time seemed suspended. She knew her imagination had a lot to answer for when Carter took a step to the side and, placing a hand beneath her elbow, suggested easily, 'I'd better take you around and introduce you before some of these Frenchmen start to stampede over here.'

It was flattering being introduced to so many males who complimented her with their eyes. But her interest was only for the man she was with. Though, because she'd realised from Carter's 'You'll definitely be needed at lunch' that her role had to be in her PR capacity, she was friendly with everyone she came into contact with—and that included a thirtyish, fresh sort of man who ogled more than he complimented.

She saw Carter frown, and she tried to cover his displeasure by being extra friendly. They were there to negotiate business but, given that she hadn't a clue what that business was, it seemed to her there was more chance of a favourable outcome if she was friendly to the opposition.

So she smiled and chatted, and somehow got separated from Carter. She saw Solène, waved, and thought Solène looked absolutely superb in her new outfit. She saw from the sign Solène made that Solène thought the same about her and her new outfit. Then Ashlyn greeted Luc—and spotted Carter in conversation with an animated beauty; she was then able to recognise that peculiar sensation she had last felt in her stomach ages ago for what it was. She was jealous.

'You will sit by me, Ashlyn, for your lunch, yes?' enquired the one man whom she wasn't too keen on.

She looked to Carter; he was hanging on the animated beauty's every word. 'I'd love to,' she smiled at Mr Ogle-eyes, fully aware that if Carter wanted her nearer he would do something about it.

But quite clearly Carter had no need of her. In no time she was seated with Mr Ogle-eyes on one side and a rather pleasant man who reminded her of her cousin Teddy on the other.

Ashlyn strove desperately hard to keep her eyes away from that part of the table where Carter Hamilton was sitting. He was entirely oblivious to the woman he had earlier thought 'stunning'—fickle swine! She passed her lunchtime trying to make it appear as if she was deeply interested in what the men on either side of her had to say.

She had been introduced to so many people by then that although she usually had a good memory for names her 'name bank' was fast being used up. She was in luck, though: both the man on her right and the one on the left were called Matthieu. Sometimes life was made easier—and Carter was *still* talking to *that woman*!

'You are in Paris for long?'

Ashlyn tuned in to realise that Matthieu Ogle-eyes had asked her a question. 'Regretfully only for a few days,' she replied.

'Perhaps I may show you a little of Paris this evening?' That came from Matthieu on her other side.

'That was what I was going to ask!' Matthieu Ogle-eyes protested, clearly put out.

Ashlyn laughed, and it seemed to cool the situation. She looked to see what Carter was doing, and saw that he was looking—no, not looking, but glowering—at her. Now what had she done?

Feeling unnerved, she turned back to her two companions. 'May I?' the nice Matthieu persisted—and somehow she remembered he had asked her out that evening.

'It's very kind of you to ask me, but I'm here with Mr Hamilton, and I'm not sure what our itinerary is for this evening.'

'Shall I have your phone number?' Matthieu Ogle-eyes asked. Not a hope! 'I will ring you later, and we can arrange—'

'I'm so sorry, I don't know what our number is,' she replied, and just didn't believe it when both of them dived into their wallets and extracted their personal cards.

'Perhaps you'll ring me if you are free,' the nice Matthieu said.

'I'll do my best,' she responded diplomatically, turning from one Matthieu to the other, and slipping their cards into the tiny pocket of her jacket. 'Have both of you always lived in Paris?' she asked, and the remainder of lunch was spent hearing a great deal about what was best to see in the city.

That lunch seemed to be the longest Ashlyn had ever lived through, so that she wasn't at all surprised, when the party started to break up, to see that it was getting on for five.

Carter was at last on his own—put the flags out! Or, at least, *she* wasn't there. He was standing in conversation with Luc and Solène. He looked over to her—and she felt frost in the air!

He made no move to come over, so clearly he expected her to go to him. She was of the opinion that he could go take a running jump—then looked down at her suit. Ultimately he paid her salary—she wasn't sure how she felt about being 'employed'—and the nasty Matthieu Ogle-eyes was starting to be a little tedious.

'If you'll excuse me,' she smiled, shaking hands with both Matthieus.

'I shall look forward to your phone call, Ashlyn.'

'And I.'

'*Au revoir,*' she bade them, and, determined not to hurry, she went sedately over to where Carter was just saying goodbye to his friends.

She joined them, saying her goodbyes too. Then she and Carter were outside, getting into a taxi, and he was snarling, 'I take it you enjoyed your lunch?'

Not so well as you! 'It was superb, wasn't it?' she beamed. A grunt was her answer.

When they arrived at their destination she left him paying the taxi driver and went into the apartment block. Was it always going to hurt like this? Loving him like crazy, yet, at the same time, wanting to crash something heavy and painful down on his head?

She had composed her expression by the time Carter joined her in the lift. It was a silent journey upwards. Once inside the apartment she went straight to her room. He did not try to stop her.

Oh, Lord, she was here with him until, perhaps, Friday. Possibly three more days. Three more un- bearable days. She was past analysing what had gone wrong and got out of her suit and went and took a shower.

A few minutes later she stepped out of the shower and, with her hair loose down her back, she donned a robe. She wished, and didn't wish, that she hadn't kissed him back last night.

She acknowledged that he'd got her so mixed-up she couldn't think straight. He'd got her emotions into such an uproar that she seemed constantly on a see-saw, wanting to laugh at something he said one minute, feeling like crying the next.

Well, she wouldn't— A knock suddenly sounded on her door and for a couple of seconds she panicked and wasn't capable of thinking of anything. Quickly she got herself together. Unmistakably Carter wanted her for something, regardless of the fact that she could be in any state of undress, or without a stitch on for that matter! He wasn't the sort to wait too patiently—or, in her case, too politely either.

Visualising him coming in at any moment, Ashlyn tightened the belt of her thin robe—her only covering—and went and opened the door. Only then, as she saw him make a thorough if rapid study of her long hair loose about her shoulders, her curvaceous but thinly clad, slender body, before his glance came swiftly back to her face, did she recall that she wasn't wearing a scrap of make-up. Oh, great! And there was he, dressed up like a dog's dinner in an immaculate suit, crisp white shirt, showered and shaven.

'Yes!' she snapped—why wouldn't she? Nothing like the man you loved seeing you when you knew you weren't looking your best!

He was not happy with her tone, she could tell. Tough! 'I've a business appointment,' he informed her sharply. So that was what they called it! 'It's unlikely I'll be back to take you to dinner.'

As if she'd go! 'Good heavens, I've not long finished lunch—I couldn't eat another thing!' she exclaimed.

'There's food in the—'

'Have a good time—with your business!' she bade him, and closed her door—and wished with all she had that she hadn't added that last bit. Had there been a note of jealousy there? Had Carter picked it up? Oh, heavens, she did hope not.

Ashlyn went and sat down, aware that if Carter, with his quick intelligence, was not going to glean how she felt about him she was going to have to be much more careful in future.

A few minutes later, however, her pride was up in arms again. If he was truly going out on 'business', why couldn't he take her with him? She was there because he 'needed a board member' with him, wasn't she? Lying toad!

Well, if he thought she was staying home to have a quiet evening in while he was out on the town wining and dining his French lady-friend—she didn't need two guesses to know that he had fixed that evening's date with her at lunchtime—he had another think coming! She'd had the offer of a date at lunchtime too. Two of them in fact.

Without more ado Ashlyn went and found the cards the two Matthieus had given her. Matthieu Boirel and Matthieu Litique. Both had suggested she phone them—but which was which?

She recalled the nice Matthieu, the one like her cousin Teddy; but, if she'd heard his surname, she could not remember it. She then thought of the other Matthieu. She hadn't taken to him at all.

Oh, she wouldn't go! Yes, she would. She had a fifty per cent chance of getting the Matthieu who had seemed harmless. She wasn't going to sit in while Carter was out tom-catting!

She shuffled the cards and took them over to the phone. Matthieu Boirel's card was the top one. She dialled his number. '*Allô. C'est* Ashlyn Ain—' She did not have to say more.

'*Ashlyn! Chérie!*' Matthieu Boirel exclaimed—and she knew at once that she had got the wrong Matthieu!

After her phone call Ashlyn went and took stock of her wardrobe. Matthieu had spoken of them going to a nightclub. Ashlyn, with silent thanks for her mother's foresight, decided on the gold dress with the narrow shoulder-straps.

Recalling the way Matthieu Boirel had ogled her at lunchtime, she was not, in all honesty, looking forward to the evening she had arranged with him. But each time she thought of putting through an urgent call to cancel she thought of Carter *expecting* her to stay placidly in the apartment while he went off amusing himself. Besides, she had no idea, bearing in mind she had met Matthieu at a business lunch, if any last-minute cancellation she made might be detrimental to any business Carter had in mind.

Well, she hoped, hoped, hoped that Carter would be at the same nightclub where she and Matthieu planned to be that night. It would give her enormous pleasure to thumb her nose at him—he with his 'There's food in the—' Let him eat it!

In the event she did not see Carter at the nightclub Matthieu Boirel took her to. In fact it was so dark in there, until her eyes became accustomed to what light there was, she felt she could have been sitting at a table next to her long-lost aunt and never have known it!

Not that any aunt of Ashlyn's would frequent such a place! Ashlyn owned that she had never been to a club quite like it. Matthieu had called for her before time; the concierge had telephoned her to say Monsieur Boirel was there. She'd opted not to have him sent up. Pausing only to drape her matching stole about her, she'd picked up her evening bag and gone down to greet him.

The moment she'd got into his car and he'd 'accidentally' placed his hand on her knee, she'd known that she had made a mistake in arranging to see him. But, when she'd firmly removed his hand and he'd murmured, *'Pardon,'* she'd thought she could handle him.

She began to have her doubts about that, though, as the evening in the dingy little club wore on. He did not offer her anything to eat—not that she wanted anything—but he tried hard to ply her with drink. Ashlyn stuck firmly with the one she had.

They were seated on a bench type of seat. Matthieu moved closer and put an arm along the back. She moved away. Other couples were dancing—at least she could make out outlines of couples moving to the sound of music coming from somewhere.

'Shall we dance?' Matthieu asked.

It seemed a good idea. If she moved any further away from him, she'd fall off the end of the seat. 'That would be nice,' she consented, thinking that she must try and spread herself away from him when they got back. Encouragement he did not need: it soon became clear that dancing with him was not a good idea after all. He held her too close and she felt she was suffocating.

She took a hold of his waist, intending to push him away. He got the wrong idea and grabbed her more firmly. Business or no business, it was time to tell him to get lost.

Ashlyn then thought that he had got the message anyway, because he breathed in her ear, 'Shall we go?'

It was the best thing he'd said all night. 'Please,' she said—and was never more grateful to be out in the fresh air.

Any feeling of relief she experienced, however, was short-lived, because she soon discovered that, while they spoke each other's verbal language perfectly, they were on different planets when it came to body language.

For they had been driving less than five minutes back to her apartment, or so she thought, when Matthieu Boirel turned the car into a side-street, stopped the engine and, with an urgent, 'I can't wait any longer,' made a lunge for her.

Ashlyn was just not ready for it. In no time flat he had her pinned beneath him, his loose mouth seeking hers. It was then that she came rapidly to life. Carter's mouth was the last mouth to touch hers and she wasn't having that wonderful memory sullied by this oaf.

'No!' she yelled. *'Non!'* But Matthieu Boirel took no notice.

The next few minutes were a complete and utter nightmare as she fought against what seemed to be this man's maniacal desire for her. He just would not listen to her pleas to leave her alone. Which left her terrified, gulping for air when she had the chance, and fighting and kicking like fury whenever she was able.

His face was near, so she bit it, and kept on biting until, with a yell of rage, he let her go.

By some sheer magical good luck she found the door-catch, and she was out of the car while he was still holding his face, out of the car and running, running, crossing streets, and still running.

Ashlyn slowed down only when her frequent glances behind showed her she was not being followed. She had no idea where she was, or what the time was. Then, by sheer good fortune, she saw a taxi heading her way—but she was in such shock by then that she didn't care whether it was taken or not—or even if it ran her over.

She went swiftly into the street and stood in the middle of the road waving her arms. The taxi screeched to a halt, the driver grumbling like fury. She got into the taxi and, striving for all the dignity she could manage, given that her hair was a mess and Lord knew what her make-up was like, she gave him the address of the apartment.

The taxi moved off and she felt too exhausted to worry that she did not have her bag, which she had left behind in her rush to escape Matthieu Boirel's car. The concierge could pay; she would pay the concierge back later, or Hamilton Holdings would. She didn't seem to be thinking straight, and felt like bursting into tears when the taxi driver pulled up outside the apartment block.

Managing to hold back tears, she asked the concierge to pay and give a generous tip. Seeming astonished that this usually im-maculate-looking young woman should return in such a state, he assured her that he would.

As well as having no money, she had no doorkey. But that didn't bother her either. If Carter wasn't in she would park herself outside the apartment door. At least here she felt safe.

Carter was in. She rang the bell. It was answered immediately. He was still up, dressed in shirt and trousers—and he was furious!

'Where the hell have you been?' he bellowed before he'd barely shut the door.

Ashlyn, feeling closer to tears than ever, was afraid to speak lest she break down and start sobbing. Unable to speak, she rushed past him. But, as she might have known, he wasn't having that.

He followed her to her room, turning on the main light as he came in. In that strong light and not the table-lamp glow of the sitting room, he saw for the first time her ashen face and her shocked look.

'What happened?' he demanded to know at once.

'I went out with Matthieu Boirel; he——'

'Alone?' Carter barked, clearly knowing at once who Matthieu Boirel was.

'Yes,' she answered wearily, wishing Carter would go. She wanted to forget it; she didn't need this third degree. She turned away, realising that by some miracle she still had her stole about her. Perhaps she'd straightened it in the taxi; she couldn't remember. She took it off, wanting to go to bed, wanting to go to sleep, wanting to pretend that it had never happened.

Then she noticed, as Carter at once noticed, that both the straps of her dress were broken and hanging down, and that her arms were red and starting to bruise.

'What in God's name has happened to you?' Carter thundered, enraged——his fury was back with a vengeance!

CHAPTER EIGHT

ASHLYN was glad to hear fury in Carter's voice. It made her begin to get angry too—and saved her from tears. She had done nothing wrong that she could think of, except maybe been a little too proud. But she hadn't deserved Matthieu Boirel's assault on her, and she did not deserve Carter bellowing at her now, either.

'I got attacked, that's what happened!' she flew at him, glad of her anger, glad of her fury.

'Who by?' Carter blazed. 'Boirel? Did he...?'

'No! All he managed to do was to scare me half to death!' she charged. 'I got away.'

'Where is he?' To her amazement she saw that Carter was boiling over with outrage—but not for her! His expression was violent—he looked ready to kill Matthieu Boirel! She could only put it down to shock that his doing so seemed quite a good idea.

Somehow her anger was neutralised. 'I left him in his car in some side-street,' she answered. 'With any luck he's still nursing a badly bitten face.'

'You bit him?'

'As hard as I could! I'd hoped I was ringing Matthieu Litique,' she felt she should explain, 'but—'

'You rang and asked Boirel out?' Carter looked astounded.

'What if I did?' This was all she needed— for Carter to know she'd been so miffed when he'd gone out for the evening that she had decided to go out too. 'They both asked me out at lunchtime and gave me their cards, only I didn't know which one was which and rang the wrong one and...' Her voice tailed off. Carter was looking angry with her again.

'You're not safe to be let out!' he stated shortly, but she had had enough.

'Leave me be!' she shouted, furious again. She didn't know where she was when Carter came and took hold of her arms. 'And cut that out!' she raged, distraught, not thinking properly. 'I've just been through that! I w-want comfort—n-not r-rape!'

Carter looked at her, thunderstruck. Then, 'Dammit,' he groaned, and she realised that his hold had been more to steady her than anything else when she'd started shouting. He came closer, and gently, tenderly, he eased her into the cradle of his arms. 'I wouldn't rape you, little one,' he soothed, and placed a whisper of a kiss in her hair.

How long she stood there shaking, being gently held by him, she had no idea. Tears came to her eyes and spilled over, and she didn't seem able to stop them. She felt ashamed of crying, ashamed of what had happened to her, ashamed—and mixed-up.

Nor did she want to look at Carter when, after long, long minutes of him just holding her safe, he drew back to look into her face, possibly to gauge if she was any better.

'Oh, little darling,' he breathed when he saw her tear-stained face. Ashlyn had never known a man's touch could be so sensitive when, having led her to the bathroom, he sat her down and tenderly sponged her face and oh, so considerately dried it.

And Ashlyn wanted to cry again. Because had this not happened to her she would never have imagined that Carter could be so sensitive, so caring. Not that he truly cared—it was surely just that he was there and she seemed in need of someone's help and he was the one available.

'I'm all right now,' she told him bravely as a modicum of pride began to stir.

'You look it,' he smiled, and was as ever in charge as he asserted, 'Come on, let's get you to bed.'

He helped her from the bathroom, and she hated him a little because it was clear he knew where to find a woman's nightdress when he pushed a hand under her pillow and retrieved hers. She was all at sixes and sevens, though, when, after bringing her nightdress over to her, his hands went to the zip at the side of her dress.

Anxiously she jerked away. 'I c-can manage now,' she stammered, backing from him, her head a nonsense as shock from her experience with Matthieu Boirel clashed with a tingle of awareness of Carter's touch to her skin.

'Steady—steady,' he gentled her. 'I didn't mean to—' He broke off, and then instructed evenly, 'Get into bed. I'll go and see if I can find you a couple of aspirin.'

'I don't want asp—' Why was she arguing?

Carter's look was kind, but he was still the one in charge when calmly he cut in to tell her, 'It's either that or I call a doctor.'

'Oh, really!' she flared impatiently.

'Aspirin or doctor?'

Swine! 'Aspirin.'

'Have much to drink?' he enquired easily before he went.

She shook her head. 'One gin and tonic—and I didn't finish all of that.' Her voice had started to wobble as she remembered. 'And I don't want to talk about it.'

His expression softened. 'Get into bed, there's a love.' He left her to go searching for aspirin.

Ashlyn, as instructed, was in bed when Carter returned. He came over, placed a glass of water on the bedside table and switched on the small bedside lamp. Then he turned off the centre light. Ashlyn found that softer light comforting, and obediently sat up and swallowed two aspirins when Carter handed her the glass of water.

Then he took it from her and placed it on the bedside table again. 'Lie down,' he instructed. 'You'll be all right now. I'm not far away if—if you get uneasy.'

Just his understanding alone was comforting, but when Ashlyn went to lie down she suddenly felt agitated and struggled back up again. 'I—can't,' she said breathlessly, a kind of panic overtaking her.

'Little love,' Carter breathed, and, sitting down on the side of her bed, he reached for her. 'Come here,' he said. His arms came around her, and again, for long minutes, he held her. 'Shh—you're all right,' he murmured gently.

'I can't stop shaking,' she told him.

'I know. Don't worry about it. You'll be fine.' He pulled back and looked into her wide green eyes. 'Come on,' he coaxed with a smile. 'You need some rest, some sleep.'

He was right and she knew it. Ashlyn moved out of his arms and lay down, and immediately wanted his arms back. 'Don't go,' she heard her voice whisper, barely aware that she was speaking.

And she knew no end of relief when he teased, 'Would I?' She smiled. She loved him. She closed her eyes—and panicked once more. Her eyes shot wide. 'I'm here,' he reassured her quickly, reading the fear in the worried green depths of her eyes.

'Carter. Carter,' she said urgently. 'W-would you kiss me?'

He looked at her, studied her, and she loved him because he seemed to know just why she wanted him to kiss her—so that she might forget the revulsion caused by that other man's mouth.

'Your wish is my command,' he said lightly. And in that same light tone he invited, 'Pucker up.' She smiled again—but tensed as he leaned over and his head came nearer. 'Just relax, sweetheart,' Carter bade her softly. 'It will all be over in less than a second.'

And it was. Simply, briefly, barely touching, his lips brushed hers, and suddenly her world righted itself. He smiled down at her, his eyes asking the question 'All right?' 'Thank you,' she told him—only that didn't seem enough. She stretched up her arms to him, wanting to hold him as he had held her. Somehow she needed to convey how grateful she was to him for spending this short time with her until she got herself back together again.

She moved, sat up a little, and while Carter was still so close she moved again. She placed her mouth against his, though not a brief brushing of mouths the way his had been. He stilled, then pulled back. 'Are we still slaying gremlins?' he wanted to know.

'I'm not sure,' she answered honestly. 'I just—want to be close to you.'

'I—er...' For the first time since she had known him, Carter looked uncertain about something. That made her love him more, made her want to comfort him, as he had comforted her.

She stretched towards him again, and placed her mouth against his, her arms going around him. She heard a kind of groan escape him, and to her delight felt his chest come against hers as he lay down with her.

'Oh, Carter,' she sighed when he broke the kiss and lay, his face barely inches from hers, looking at her.

'You're a minx, young woman,' he growled, and she laughed. He seemed pleased to at last see her growing more cheerful when she had been through a whole gamut of other emotions—including tears. As though he couldn't help himself, he gently kissed her, drawing from her her very soul in that undemanding caress.

She almost cried his name again when he broke away, but instead told him openly, 'I've never thought too much about kissing, but I really like kissing you.' And, because for once everything seemed to be right between them, she asked, 'Could I have another one, please?'

'Oh—I'm not so sure,' he began warily, and she laughed again.

'Don't be so mean—you've got plenty.'

He laughed, and she loved him, and it all seemed so unreal—and, at the same time, she had never seemed so awake, so alive and open to him. So Carter kissed her, and she held him and he held her close and when they broke from that kiss—and Carter looked at her—it seemed the most natural thing that he should kiss her again.

And again and again. Ashlyn had no idea how long they lay together with just a sheet and a blanket separating them. Kissing, being kissed, in gentle, going nowhere in a hurry pleasuring.

She had heard Carter's shoes fall to the floor some time ago, and had never known such bliss when, with the long length of his body close to hers, she melted under a long, long, tender kiss.

And yet for all their kisses were unhurried, healing, and tender, Ashlyn suddenly started to feel the need for something more. Her lips parted beneath the tenderness of Carter's sensational mouth. She felt a spasm pass through him, a different kind of awareness take him.

He pulled back. 'Ashlyn,' he breathed her name, and moved then as though to push her away. But she didn't want that and she moved too—and somehow his right hand came into contact with her left breast.

They both stilled, her eyes shooting to his. For some reason, he did not seem able to take his hand away. And for the same reason she did not want him to.

'Do—you mind?' he asked, a hoarse kind of note in his voice. Wordlessly she shook her head. 'You're not afraid?' he had to know.

She almost told him then that she loved him. 'No,' she whispered. 'I...I like you—touching me.'

'Little Ashlyn,' he breathed, and kissed her, his hand gentle on her breast.

She moved nearer to him, kissed him. Held him closer to her—and as another groan left him suddenly the tenor of his kisses subtly changed. In no time that flicker of fire he had aroused in her once before was there again, bursting into flames.

And as Carter began to tenderly mould her breast, tease the hardened tip, and trail kisses down her throat to the swell of her breasts, she knew that he desired her too.

'Carter, Carter, Carter!' She cried his name when his hand caressed inside her nightdress and she felt his warm, wonderful touch against the globe of her nakedness. 'I want to feel your skin too,' she gasped, and was shy yet unbelievably thrilled when he removed his shirt.

'Am I going too fast for you?' he asked, seeming to sense her shyness.

She shook her head, denying it, and again came close to telling him she loved him. But instead she stretched out a hand and touched his nipples. At his murmur of sound, she asked, 'Is it all right to do that?' And loved him even more when he laughed in delight at her naïvety.

'Perfectly all right,' he answered, and enquired on a teasing note, 'Would it be impertinent of me, do you suppose, if I suggested I'd like to see you without this?' He touched the cotton of her nightdress. 'As pretty as it is,' he added.

'Carter, I...'

'You're not sure?'

She panicked. If she said she wasn't sure he wouldn't make love to her any more, she just knew it. It was such bliss to be in his arms, to be with him like this—and she desired him.

She took a deep, courage-seeking breath. 'I'm positively positive,' she smiled, and was rewarded with a long and lingering kiss.

She found that Carter was not rushing to relieve her of her nightdress, but first stroked her hair, her face, and kissed her tenderly again, before, at last, his long, sensitive fingers caressed down to the neck of her nightdress. The opening was large enough for him to slip it down and away from her. His mouth was over hers as he caressed the folds down over her shoulders, his fingers lingering to tease her urgent body and her breasts. Then her night-dress was down to her waist and he was ca-ressing her slender hips, her silken thighs—and then she was naked against him.

She still felt shy, but wouldn't have had it any other way when Carter pulled her close up against him, her naked breasts coming into contact with his chest. They kissed and he sent her half-crazy when he lowered his head and kissed her right breast and tormented its hard pink tip. Then he was embracing her again, stroking, caressing, and she pressed up against him knowing that before he left he would have made complete love to her. And as the passion between them soared, to make complete love with him was what, with all her heart, she wanted.

Quite when, or how for that matter, Carter removed his trousers she had no idea. All she did know was that she had once had a night-dress, a sheet and blanket plus a pair of trousers between them, and now they were all at once no longer there.

She felt Carter's well-muscled thighs burn against her own, and in a moment of mys-terious modesty she instinctively went backwards instead of forwards. 'Shh,' he gentled her, his hands caressing and cupping her naked behind, drawing her closer, yet closer to him.

And she relaxed against him. 'Oh, Carter,' she cried, 'forgive me—I didn't mean to. It's just I've so much to learn, to...' She stopped talking and she pressed up against him. She was in a world of mindless wanting—when all of a sudden she became aware that Carter had stilled, was not moving. Correction: he was moving—away from her! 'What's wrong?' she asked urgently, hanging onto him. He was trying to get off the bed—but he mustn't.

'Let go, Ashlyn, let go!' he commanded her hoarsely.

'No!' she refused, her arms tight about him. He wanted her as she wanted him; she knew that he did. 'I...'

'For God's sake...' She felt his hands on her wrists, felt his energy as he prised her hands off him. 'It's *over*! Forget it!' he grated.

'Forget it?' she echoed, totally bewildered— what the dickens was going on?

'Go to sleep!'

'Sleep!' Was he crazy? She wanted him. He wanted her! Or did he want her? She looked at him, saw he already had his trousers back on, saw him grab for his shirt. Oh! She shook her head, trying to clear her bafflement. Carter did *not* want her!

Still she could not believe the evidence of her eyes. Even when Carter, without so much as a backward glance, hotfooted it out of her room, she still could not believe it.

But belief was only a minute or so away. For while she sat there—stark naked and stunned—she heard the sound of the door of the apartment opening and, with a determined thud, closing. Carter, unbelievably, had gone out!

Gone out! Her brain seemed to seize up for long, long moments after that. But later she would have welcomed such a numbed state of mind. Because, as her brain started to wake up, so everything became totally unendurable.

She had once thought Carter could not hurt her. But he had. And she could not take it. He had gone out. He did not want her. She had more or less invited him to make love to her. He hadn't desired her at all until she had started kissing him and had clung onto him.

Oh, how she had clung onto him! Even when it was obvious that he'd gone off the idea of making love to her, she had continued to cling onto him. He'd almost had to cut himself free!

Oh... Pink colour surged to her face. He had rejected her and, because it had looked as if she wouldn't leave him alone, he had gone out. Probably to book himself into a hotel, for all she knew.

The humiliation that came with the thought was beyond bearing. To think that, for the sake of some peace, Carter might have booked himself into other accommodation was crucifying! He would have to return in the morning for his briefcase, but... Suddenly Ashlyn knew that she would never be able to look Carter in the face again. That was when she moved.

In less than no time, her pride barely surviving the hammering of her thoughts, she was dressed, packed and on her way. She did not anticipate bumping into Carter as she rode down in the lift, nor did she.

'Ah, *madame*,' the concierge greeted her, when, complete with suitcase, she stepped out of the lift. And, evidently used to people coming in and out at all times of the day and night, he enquired, anticipating her needs, 'Taxi?'

Only then did Ashlyn recall that he had paid for her other taxi. She reimbursed him, then rode to the airport trying desperately hard to keep her mind a blank.

But how impossible that was. She needed to be busy, but she had to sit around waiting for a plane, then sit on a plane with nothing to do but go over and over how she had clung to Carter like a limpet—and how he had rejected her.

After the plane had landed, Ashlyn drove home dejected, humiliated and with Carter, Carter, Carter whirling around in her head. Which was probably why she was on the drive of her home before it all at once dawned on her that her parents would want to know why she was back. Somehow it seemed she had been away for a lifetime. Yet it hadn't even been two days!

She went in, a bright smile on her face, and found her parents in the drawing room reading the morning papers. 'Had a good trip?' her mother asked as Ashlyn bent to kiss her cheek in greeting. No 'you're back soon' or anything of that nature.

The explanation for that, however, became apparent when, going over to greet her father likewise, he beamingly relayed, 'Carter Hamilton rang to see if you were home yet. He wants you to ring him as soon as you get in.' Shaken, Ashlyn started to come out of her numbed state—like hell she'd ring him! 'I've taken down the number. Must be something important,' her father went on proudly. 'He was calling you from Paris.'

'I'll take my case up and give him a call from upstairs,' she remarked, knowing that she was lying and, because of it, looking away from her father.

Up in her room Ashlyn avoided the telephone like the plague. Carter had asked her to give him a ring once before—had it been only last Friday? Good heavens! And she had— then. 'Home safe,' she had told him, and had been happy.

Rebellion gave her a prod. He had been responsible for her being happy then, and he was responsible for her being miserable now, and she wasn't going to cry. Nor was she going to ring him. She hoped it would worry him, though of course it wouldn't.

Just a woman of easy virtue—that was all she was to him. And she could not deny it. She had invited everything that had taken place. She shouldn't still love him, but she did, and life was hell. But if he was waiting for her to ring him, then he could wait on!

What did he want her to call him for anyway? Probably so he could tell her again 'It's *over*! Forget it!' She should give him that opportunity! Never! Pride arrived in great bucket-loads, and she was never more glad of it.

She still felt humiliated beyond belief, but pride told her that she was the only one who was going to know it; pride was a great ally. Yet she was still haunted by her lack of sense last night—ye gods, she used to wonder if she was a bit staid because she had never wanted to go to bed with anybody! She'd clung to Carter like a leech!

Ashlyn did not wish to remember such things but found she spent the rest of the day fending off memories which would arrive unbidden at any second. While she was striving with all she had to forget Carter, her delighted father was forever—it seemed like every five minutes—bringing Carter's name up. In his proud view, he had been right to insist on a seat on the board for her.

'I expect Carter will want you to accompany him many more times in your diplomatic capacity now that this French trip has been so successful,' he opined over dinner. Ashlyn knew she only had to say one word in the affirmative and her father would be on the phone to his brothers.

'I do have other work,' she prevaricated, knowing that wild horses would not get her anywhere near the office of Hamilton Holdings ever again.

Though, offhand, she couldn't think of a thing she had to do. She had been engaged primarily to take Carter's messages, and only temporarily at that. But he was out of the country and... Oh, Carter, Carter, Carter!

Proof, however, that he was back in the country came as she was crossing the hall from the dining room. The phone rang.

'Hello?' she answered, thinking it to be one of the family—and almost dropped the receiver like a hot brick on hearing the well-remembered male voice at the other end.

'You're home!' Carter stated. And before she could do more than wonder why he sounded a little relieved to know that he had the outrageous audacity to add, 'I'll come over.'

He was back! In England! He wasn't due back yet! Another riot of emotions bombarded her. She selected pride. 'Suit yourself,' she answered coldly. 'I'm going out.' With that she put down the phone and, knowing from experience that he lived half an hour away at least, she raced to her room, picked up her bag, looked in on her parents to say she was meeting friends, and went quickly out to her car.

Only then did she allow other emotions to crowd in. She knew why she had bolted, of course. She was ashamed and totally unable to speak to him. What was there to say? His ringing her at home—twice—had to mean that it was personal, and from where she stood she had been more personal with him than with any other man. That was quite personal enough.

Her breath caught on a dry sob as she recalled Carter's overwhelming tenderness with her when he had sponged her face, his wonderful understanding... How he had gently coaxed her out of her shock. How they had kissed...

Hastily Ashlyn blanked her thoughts again. She didn't want to remember his goodness, his sensitivity. Turning the knife it might be, but she had to remember instead his coldness to her. His 'It's *over*!' Damn him—no man said that to her and thought he could ring up and say, 'I'll come over,' and *think* she should wait in for him!

Ashlyn welcomed her outraged pride; it got her through the next four hours. She waited until she was certain that if Carter had chanced it and called anyway he would be gone by now.

She knew the moment she turned her car into the drive and saw that there was no light on in the drawing room that Carter had not called. Had he done so, one or other of her parents, or both, would have been waiting up to tell her everything there was to tell.

'Not going to your office today?' her father enquired the next morning when she was still at the table ten minutes after she would normally have left for work.

'That's the bonus of being away—you are allowed time off when you get back,' she answered, again finding it impossible to look her father in the eye. He was so obsessed by pride—how in the world could she tell him that she was never going back?

'You know your mother and I will be out all day.'

'New carpets,' Ashlyn smiled, heartily glad of the change of subject.

'We don't need them!' he protested.

'Spend some of your money,' Ashlyn teased.

'That's what your mother said.'

The house was quiet when her parents had gone. Ashlyn realised her nerves must be getting in a state when she all but jumped out of her skin when the phone rang.

She feared to answer it. It might be him! Grief, don't be stupid, she told herself. Carter was a proud man—he wouldn't put up with a snub twice. She picked up the phone.

'Hello?' she said.

'Ash—'

'In case you haven't got the message, I don't want to talk to you!' she snapped, and knew as she slammed down the phone that that was it. Carter would not ring a third time.

And that too upset her, because, while she was too embarrassed to want to see him ever again—God, she'd been *naked* against him— at the same time she could not bear the thought of *never* seeing him again.

She did see him again, though—that morning. She was in her room when she heard a car pull onto the drive. It wasn't an engine sound she recognised. Todd took that bend as if his life depended on speed, Susannah only marginally less fast.

Ashlyn went and took a look out of the window, and her legs went like water. Tall, straight, purposeful, what was Carter doing here? He moved out of her line of vision. She heard his ring at the door. Thank goodness it was Thursday; Mrs North was out doing the shopping.

Carter rang the bell again. Ashlyn had no intention of answering it. He rang it a third and then a fourth time. Ashlyn stood immobile at the window. Carter came into her line of vision as he moved away from the door. She saw him stand there and look up at the windows. She was well to the side of the curtains, where she froze.

If he was trying to gauge if she was there, and in which room, tough! She watched him, expecting him to return to his car. She felt a fluttery sensation in her insides when he walked not to his car but away from it. Where the dickens was he going? Surely he . . . ?

She leaned forward; he had walked out of her line of vision. Oh, no—suddenly she saw that he had gone to stand and look at her car. Oh, grief, she had been late in last night and had had too much on her mind to think to put it away. Oh, heavens, Carter knew it was her car; he had seen her into it last Friday after his dinner party. Did he suspect there was a very good chance that she was in?

She watched him start to walk back to his own car then saw him look up. Hastily she pulled back—oh, drat, she'd disturbed the curtains! Had he seen? Her breath caught and she froze again. Then she was awash with relief. Albeit that there seemed something even more purposeful about him—there was determination in his every stride—Carter continued on to his car, got in and drove off.

It took Ashlyn every minute of the time before her parents returned to get herself together again.

Why in creation had Carter called? Why had he driven to her home when he should be at work? He should still be in Paris, shouldn't he? Perhaps he'd come to apologise. Ashlyn tossed that idea out. Just because his 'It's *over*! Forget it!' was seared for ever on her brain, it didn't mean that he more than passingly remembered saying it. And, anyway, he could always write—not that she'd read his letter, she thought sniffily. Then she wondered what it was she thought he might apologise for. It was she who had done all the clinging. Oh, heck, when she thought of how she had fastened herself onto him!

Her skin burned and she wanted to cry, to thump him, to be a million miles away. As it was, she stayed home, strove to keep calm, and tried to think up some excellent unarguable-with reason to explain to her father why she would not be attending another board meeting.

'I'm exhausted,' her father declared at dinner. 'Your mother is indefatigable.' The subject of carpets occupied the mealtime.

By morning, after yet another fractured night, Ashlyn knew that she was going to have to weather her father's disappointment and tell him that she didn't want to be a board member any more. Perhaps she could tell him that she'd had a personality clash with Carter—that was one name for what had happened!

In an unhappy frame of mind she went down to breakfast, wishing that there were some easy way out. If there was, she couldn't think of it.

Her father was in the breakfast room, his head in his financial newspaper. 'Hamilton Holdings are up again,' he commented by way of a good morning. 'I wonder if your uncle Edward still takes this paper now he's retired?'

Ashlyn gave an inner sigh. That pride again! He *wanted* Uncle Edward to see how well Hamilton Holdings were doing. 'I expect he does,' she said, taking her place at the table and still trying to find a painless way to convey to her father that not only would she not be going to Hamilton Holdings that morning, but that she was never going there again. A moment of courage arrived. 'Dad?' she attracted his attention. He looked up—there had been something a little strangled about her tone—and then Mrs North came into the breakfast room with the post.

'He's late this morning,' she remarked, handing a bundle of letters to her employer.

'I'll bet he didn't spend all yesterday looking at carpets,' her father grumbled, inspecting the mail the housekeeper had brought in. 'Ah, here's one for you, Ashlyn—from Hamilton's!' he exclaimed, checking the Hamilton Holdings crest. 'Now why would they be writing to you when you'll be there with them in a little while?'

Oh, grief, he was already sounding a little perturbed that something might be wrong. Her heart sank—how *could* she tell him? She couldn't face it, not then, and, her courage gone for the moment, she invented, 'Oh, I expect they thought they'd better write in case I wasn't back from France in—er—time,' and took the envelope he handed her.

Her heart began to pump like crazy. Unusually, the envelope was handwritten—and in a hand she had seen on various documents. She just knew that it was Carter's writing!

'Hadn't you better open it?' her father suggested, when she just sat staring at the envelope, stunned. 'If it's so important that they have to let you know something before you get to the office on Monday...'

'Yes, yes, of course,' she mumbled. She didn't want to open it—not here. But her father was waiting, proudly, expectantly.

She took a knife from the table, trying desperately hard to hide the fact that her fingers were shaking. Even by post, the swine could do that to her. She glanced at her father; perhaps he'd lost interest. He hadn't! His own mail ignored, he was watching and waiting for anything he might be able to pass on.

Ashlyn withdrew the single sheet of paper from its envelope, her head in a whirl. Why was Carter writing to her? *Had* he written to apologise? Surely not!

He had *not*, she discovered when she started to read; *not* was the operative word! Though first she checked the signature. As she had thought, it *was* from Carter. But not the Carter as in 'Oh, little darling', when in that Paris apartment she had cried all over him, but as in *Rat* with a capital R. This was a more formal Carter, a very much more formal Carter. In fact a downright cold, icy Carter, who in this instance signed himself, 'C. Hamilton'.

She raised her eyes to the start of his letter. 'Dear Miss Ainsworth,' he had begun. Miss Ainsworth! Ashlyn carried on reading, pink searing her skin. She didn't believe it—couldn't believe it—and read it over again.

Dear Miss Ainsworth,

I have tried several times, and without success, to tell you in person of the extra-ordinary meeting of the Hamilton Holdings board which I have called for this Friday at 11 a.m. The purpose of this meeting is to have you removed from the board for bringing the good name of the company into ill repute.

It is my intention to put to the board your disgraceful conduct while on company business in France. You must be aware that your causing deliberate, physical harm to one of our most favoured French associates cannot be tolerated. Regrettably, I shall also have to reveal how I personally experienced a certain forwardness in your behaviour. You were advised on your first day with us that we would not countenance a scandal of any kind.

I have to tell you that, rather than have a member of this board damage the reputation of Hamilton Holdings, I have no alternative but to call for your dismissal.

You may, of course, attend the meeting to state your case if you wish. I would warn you, however, that in the event that the chairman's vote is required to have you removed from the board, then I will have no hesitation in casting it.

Yours sincerely,

C. Hamilton

Sincerely! She'd kill him! How dared he? How dared he do this to her? His nerve! His unmitigated gall! *Her* disgraceful conduct! What about *his* conduct? Scandal!

Of course she'd deliberately set about Matthieu Boirel! Of course she'd bitten him— it was the only way she could get free of that foul octopod. What was she supposed to have done?

So, OK, apart from telling Carter she had bitten the oaf, she hadn't been able to talk about it at the time. But Carter knew *why* she had bitten him. He had understood, been kind, been ...

And now, because she had responded to that rat's kindness ... True, she had asked him to kiss her, but she had thought he knew why— so she could try and banish from her thoughts the hateful memory of Matthieu Boirel's mouth. And now Carter had the outrageous nerve to tell the *whole* board just how ardently she had responded. Him and his 'a certain forwardness in your behaviour'! Glory, he wanted chopping up into little pieces and feeding to the sharks—though why poison the sharks?

'It looks to be serious, dear?'

Oh, grief, she'd forgotten her father. Serious! That was a mild term for what it was! It was one thing to want to be off the board of Hamilton Holdings, but quite another to be *thrown* off *and* in *this* way!

She looked at her father over the top of her letter. And suddenly the whole welter of implications that her dismissal from the board would arouse began to assault her, and she knew that she had to protect him. Even while she was still choking on the fact that Carter was about to tell the fourteen other male members of the board about 'a certain forwardness in her behaviour', Ashlyn knew she just couldn't sit still and take it!

Oh, Lord, someone, some female, would be there at that meeting this morning to take down the minutes. Minutes! Minutes that would have to be typed up. Minutes which, since Carter's trusted Lorna Stokes was still away, could be read by anyone in that PA's office. Ashlyn swallowed as she realised that those minutes would have to be put on file so that an auditor—or just about anybody—could have access to them. Heavens above, they were bound to get leaked to the newspapers. They'd love to know about someone being thrown off the Hamilton Holdings board—and why.

Ye gods, Uncle Edward would know about it, and Uncle Richard—not to mention the rest of the family. What about her father's pride then?

That instant Ashlyn was on her feet. 'Sorry, Dad, can't stop,' she said, waving her letter for his benefit. 'I've some urgent business to conduct.' With that, pausing only to pick up her bag and car keys, she was on her way.

She had known from the start that Carter planned to get her out as soon as he could, and on whatever pretext. Oh, how could she ever have lost sight of that?

CHAPTER NINE

ASHLYN was still furious when she parked her car at Hamilton Holdings. Getting out, she strove for calm by taking a short walk around the parking area. But only for her fury to turn to outrage when she spotted the car that had been briefly parked on her drive yesterday. Right! The scheming, despotic toad was in!

Marching straight over to the lift, she stabbed at the top-floor button. Calm—no chance! If he thought she would quietly stand by and let him do that to her father did *he* have another think coming!

Ashlyn went charging from the lift to Carter Hamilton's office. She had been there once before. That time she had knocked. This time—forget that! She went storming in.

He was there behind his desk, giving some instruction to a PA she knew, who was busy with a notepad. Ashlyn's resolve faltered a trifle. She had thought she would never be able to look him in the face again—it wasn't easy. Then he looked up to see who had entered his domain so unceremoniously. Their eyes met, and she thought he looked about to smile. But he was a treacherous rat—and her resolve came back full force. *Laugh* at her, would he?

'I want a word with you, Hamilton!' she snapped. That took the smile off his face!

He was cool, though—she'd give him that. Totally unflurried, unflustered, he instructed the startled PA, 'If you'd get on with this and...' his glance went back to Ashlyn '...see to it that I'm not disturbed for...' he paused '...an hour.' An hour! This wasn't going to take that long!

'Yes, Mr Hamilton,' the woman replied dutifully, and went quickly out.

'So you finally did it!' Ashlyn went on the attack, barely waiting for the door to close.

'Did what?' Carter was on his feet, moving over to her.

'You know damn well *what*!' she raged, wanting so desperately to be as cool as he was. But, as he came closer, she felt herself growing more agitated than ever.

'Take a seat,' he suggested, ignoring the upright one by the desk and indicating one of the 'visitor's' sofas.

'I've no intention of making myself comfortable. I'm not staying that long!' she exploded pithily, backing away from him a little. Though of course she wasn't in the least bit afraid of him, of his touch—oh, damn! She made herself think of her father. 'You've wanted me out from day one!' she challenged hotly. 'You've just been waiting for your chance since then!' She was gathering up a fine head of steam. 'Whatever flimsy pretext presented itself, you were prepared to use. You—'

'Flimsy pretext?' he echoed. Oh, Lord, clearly he didn't think the way she had clung onto him was flimsy! In truth, neither did she. But then, to her utter amazement, he added, 'You call the fact that bastard assaulted you flimsy?'

Ashlyn's jaw dropped. 'Just a minute!' she halted him. She needed time; she'd got something wrong here. So, OK, take it steady. She had been thinking of the way she and Carter... the way she had... But Carter—in very aggressive terms, she would have said— was referring to Matthieu Boirel's attack on her. Some of the heat went from her anger. 'What's going on?' she was forced to ask.

Carter's look softened at her obvious bewilderment. 'What's going on is that I desp— um—I needed to see you, but when you refused to speak to me over the phone—see me or come down from your bedroom to answer the door yesterday—' oh, grief, he *had* seen the curtains move '—I realised I was going to have to take some drastic action.'

'I . . . I'm not . . .' She couldn't fathom it.

'You've heard about Mohammed?'

'And his mountain,' she agreed.

'So I had to employ it—in reverse.'

'You came to me, but I wouldn't see you,' Ashlyn worked out slowly. 'So you decided that . . .' She looked at him, startled. 'You decided that I should come to you?'

He nodded. 'And you did. I knew in Paris that I'd hurt you,' he went on, and Ashlyn started to get seriously worried. 'But how the hell was I to make you feel any better if you wouldn't see me?'

'You shouldn't have bothered your condescending head about it!' she tossed at him loftily.

'Condescending? My G—' He broke off. 'You've no idea what you're talking about,' he told her curtly.

'Good, let's have a row!' she fired, and could have murdered him when, after a startled moment, he began to laugh.

'Oh, it's so good to see you again,' he groaned, and for one dreadfully weak moment she almost thought he meant it.

Backbone arrived, and how she needed it! 'That's why you intended having me thrown off the board, is it?'

'I'd need a far more watertight reason to have you dismissed than the one I wrote in my letter.'

'You . . .' Her voice faded. She was having a hard time taking in everything. 'I'll admit I'm growing a bit confused—but are you seriously telling me now that I'm here that you don't, after all, intend to get me thrown off?'

Carter looked at her steadily, not a glimmer of a laugh or so much as a smile about him now. 'You're here, as you've just said,' was his only comment.

But she wasn't going to leave it there. 'We're back to Mohammed and his mountain again?'

'I drove away from your home furious with you, frustrated beyond bearing,' he revealed. 'In my fury, my frustration, not to mention the fact that I was determined to see you sooner rather than later, I went over everything you and I had ever said to each other.'

Oh, heavens! 'Thorough!' she threw in, starting to feel totally mixed-up, rather than merely confused. She hadn't quite told him that she loved him but she reckoned that, by her actions, she had come pretty jolly close. She began to wish she had never come. Never left her safe home and come here.

He bore her hostility well. 'Thoroughness paid off, didn't it?'

Clever devil! She supposed by that he meant because his letter had infuriated her so much she had raced here to give him a piece of her mind. She had lost sight of that. She opened her mouth to get started, only Carter beat her to it.

'I remembered what you'd said about your father's pride in your being an executive director. Pride, obviously, in your being a member of the board. I remembered *your* pride too, remembered the way you stood up to me whenever you felt the need. I had to find some way to get you here. Believe me, Ashlyn, had there been another way, I'd have taken it.'

'Too kind!' she retorted, utterly foxed and wanting to know where this was leading.

'But, as I saw it yesterday,' he went on, ignoring her acid, 'I had few options. Should I try this, should I try that? How about if I dismissed you from the board—or threatened to? I had to dream up a set of diabolical reasons that you, with your quick intelligence, would soon realise the Press might get hold of. Things you'd fear your father might see. From what I knew of you, I knew you'd fight—if not for yourself, then for your father.'

Ashlyn stared at him, her eyes going wide, not only because of what he had said, but also because of the accuracy of his thoughts about her. Oh, heavens, if he knew that much about her, about how she felt about her father, did he know how she felt about *him*?

'You look rather shaken,' Carter went on kindly. 'Do sit down.'

'I'm not in the least shaken,' she lied haughtily. She dithered about whether to go or stay. But when Carter took another step closer, effectively blocking her way to the door—and she took a step back and felt a sofa against her legs—it seemed a good idea to sit down. 'So tell me about it!' she invited waspishly, watching him warily when he came and sat down on the arm of the sofa. 'So I'm here, apparently not to be thrown off the board because I deliberately physically harmed Matthieu Boirel. So w—?'

'I can hardly have you dismissed from the board for that reason,' Carter stated, and very nearly floored her when he added, 'Especially when I afterwards took pleasure in harming him myself.'

Ashlyn's eyes went saucer-wide. 'You hit him?' she gasped.

Carter shrugged. 'It didn't solve anything, but it certainly made me feel a whole lot better.'

Ashlyn was still staring at him in astonishment. 'You—went to see him—before you came home on—Wednesday?' Good grief, had Carter done that—for her? Surely not! No! Don't be ridiculous.

'I went to see him that night—Tuesday—after I'd left you,' Carter corrected her.

But Ashlyn, hurriedly getting herself together, decided she didn't want him thinking—and certainly not talking—about Tuesday night.

'Oh, well,' she mumbled offhandedly—and found it a wasted effort, because Carter continued anyway.

Though it was as if he was choosing his words very carefully when he stated, 'I left you that night not because I wanted to, but because I had to.'

'Pfff!' she scoffed, putting in overtime on her offhand manner. 'It's of no consequence.'

Carter didn't like that, she could tell, though whether it was what she'd said or because of her uninterested manner she couldn't decide. What she could sense—and it worried her— was that he was determined not to leave the events of Tuesday night alone. It seemed churlish—not to say too revealing—to let him know that she needed no reminding of anything. She was word- and memory-perfect about that night.

'At the risk of seeming a trifle ungallant, Ashlyn,' he went on, after a few moments of studying her and causing her to wish quite desperately that she knew what he was thinking, 'I must contradict you. It is of consequence. And I think you're lying when you deny—' It was time to go. Ashlyn moved and Carter broke off, on his feet at the same time that she was on hers. He got to the door before her.

'Let me by!' she snapped.

'After all the trouble I've had getting you here?' He shook his head. 'Not likely.'

'You're a lying toad!'

'We've both done our share.'

Ashlyn stared into dark grey eyes that had never looked more determined. 'So we'll call it quits—I'm off!' She went to go round the side of him, and found as he turned that that way was blocked. Worse, he caught hold of her upper arms. Oh, goodness—just that, and her legs went like jelly. 'Take your hands off me!' she ordered.

'I will if you'll stay.'

'Why should I?' she offered belligerently.

'Because...' He seemed to hesitate, then went on, 'Because I've something to say that—that's important to me—and I hope to you too.'

'You're never going to offer me *your* job?'

He smiled—she hadn't even dented him. Though what he then said dented her! 'What I want to say to you has nothing to do with work,' he replied. 'It's personal, between you and me.'

Oh, heavens—she couldn't take this. But from where she was standing there did not seem to be another choice. 'No doubt you've got a whole string of other lies lined up!' was the best she could manage.

'I promise you, Ashlyn, that I shall not lie to you ever again.' Oh, grief, he sounded so deadly serious and she was so weak where he was concerned. But she mustn't be weak. She had to be strong. 'Will you in return promise not to lie to me again?' he asked.

'Yes,' she lied.

Whether he believed her or not she did not know, but he let go of one of her arms and led her back to the sofa. She supposed it was because of his weakening grip, coupled with the fact that she was already at sixes and sevens, that she allowed him to do it. Not that he had looked likely to let her from the room.

Disturbingly, though, this time when Carter sat down it was not on the arm of the sofa as before, but next to her on the cushioned seat. To her mind, that was much too close.

'So what's so important that you had to lie to get me here in the first place?' she challenged, starting to become aware that if she was to get out of this with any dignity, then she had better go on the attack. To go on the defensive would be much too weakening.

'You wouldn't have come otherwise,' he excused. 'You intended never to come here again.'

She wanted to shrug, to scoff, but Carter was holding her eyes with his own. Frighteningly, though she had been prepared to lie her head off, if need be, she now discovered that she could not lie to him even about the smallest thing. 'That's right,' she agreed, and did not like one tiny bit the helpless feeling that being compelled to tell him the truth gave her. 'But we weren't talking about me,' she reminded him sharply.

'It's all connected,' he answered, somewhat obscurely, and Ashlyn was suddenly too panicky to want to ask for an explanation.

'I'm sure,' she muttered. She forced herself to go on the attack again. 'So if Matthieu Boirel is such a "favoured associate", why go and thump him?'

'You think I should have allowed him to get away with what he tried on you?'

My stars, he sounded protective! She liked it—and must not like it. 'I'm asking the questions here!' she retorted, and was little short of amazed that Carter let her get away with that.

He added to her amazement when he replied evenly, 'And I'm prepared to answer every one of those questions, Ashlyn.' She just looked at him, speechless. 'I left you that night, as I said, because I had to,' he continued.

'Go on,' she pressed hurriedly—the sooner they drew a veil over that the better.

'I admit I wasn't thinking very clearly once I got out on the street. All I knew for certain was that I wanted with everything I had in me to come back to you. But my head told me that I must not.'

'Oh?' Ashlyn tried to sound offhand again, only this time it didn't quite come off, and her voice came out sounding all husky, and nothing at all like the way she wanted it. Carter, hearing her, seemed to be encouraged. Though why he should feel the need for encouragement she wasn't sure.

'I sorely needed to get my head together,' he revealed, with a trace of a smile. 'I purposely made myself pound the pavements and stay away from you—I just couldn't think straight while I was in the same apartment with you,' he confessed.

Ashlyn's mouth fell open a fraction. 'Oh,' she murmured again. She was so shaken by what he had just said that she sat there riveted, totally forgetting that she had wanted to leave. 'Er—did you get your head straight—on your walk, I mean?'

'Only in so far as I went back over every- thing that had taken place that night.' Ashlyn suddenly decided that she wanted him to stop right there. Then she discovered that she had no need to get agitated, because Carter had traced events back to the time before she had asked him to kiss her. 'That was when I started to be furiously angry with Matthieu Boirel. That was when I grew so outraged because he had caused your tears. There was nothing I could do then but go and find him.'

'You knew where he lived?' Ashlyn put in, her heart drumming. She told herself that Carter was a gentleman, so it was quite natural he'd be outraged that some oaf had caused a woman to cry; the fact that she was that woman had nothing in particular to do with it.

'By then I did. I'd finished my business in record time.' So he *had* been out on business as he'd said. 'I'd thought you and I might go and have a look at the Paris nightlife,' Carter revealed ruefully. 'Which just showed me where I got off. You weren't waiting around, I discovered, but were already out sampling it.'

'You knew where I was?'

Carter shook his head. 'I'd no idea. All I had to go on, as I prowled around that apartment looking for clues, were a couple of cards you'd left by the telephone. I tried both numbers before putting the cards in my pocket. Both men were out. But later, when the need to flatten Boirel became more than I could withstand, I at least had his address.'

'Was he—er—surprised to see you?'

'Unfortunately he didn't know much about it.'

'You punched him one?'

'Twice. One for me and one for you. He didn't get up the second time.'

'And—um—you felt better for doing it, you said.'

'Much better. Though it solved nothing, and I returned to the apartment—'

'Did you?' she exclaimed, and quite without thinking she went on, 'I thought you were so keen to get away from me that you'd gone and booked into a hotel for the night.'

'You thought that?' he exclaimed. 'Oh, love.' He seemed not to know he had used that small endearment, but was infinitely understanding. 'No wonder you weren't there when I got back. You were hurt and feeling far more humiliated than I realised.'

But that put them into territory which Ashlyn was far too nervous to explore. 'When did you know that I'd gone home?' she asked quickly. He'd called her 'love' before, she remembered, and it had meant nothing to him then. 'That night?'

'Not until the morning,' Carter corrected her. 'I'd come back in the early hours and listened at your door in case you were having screaming nightmares over Boirel's assault on you. I didn't know then that you weren't there. I went quietly to my room to have an hour's rest. That was as much as I got, but by the time I was up, shaved and showered everything was clearer in my mind. I came to your room, cup of tea in hand, hoping to start the day right so that, hopefully, I might later have a talk with you—the talk,' he added deliberately, 'we're having here and now.'

Ashlyn swallowed, and was suddenly too stewed up inside to be able to cope with the here and now. 'You rang my home—before I got there,' she said in a rush.

'Your case had gone, the wardrobe was empty, and the concierge told me you'd taken a taxi to the airport.' Carter explained, making her realise he must truly have been concerned about her. 'It was still a tremendous relief, though, when I flew back and rang you again—and heard your lovely voice. I knew your spirit was back when you told me you were going out; there was no sign of any lingering trauma after your experience with Boirel. I realised then, and with the utmost relief, that not only were you safe, but that you would be able to cope.'

'You—er—seem to have thought about me—um—a lot,' Ashlyn said in a strangled voice.

Carter looked at her steadily and she refused to look away. Even if her insides were playing havoc, she just could not look away. And then her insides didn't merely play havoc, but gave

her the very devil, when quietly Carter revealed, 'My dear, I've thought of little else but
you since half past twelve last Tuesday when
you walked into that French hotel and stood in
the doorway. You were completely unaware that
all eyes were upon you.'

'Really!' she choked, admonishing herself to
keep her head. His 'My dear' belonged in the
same stable as 'Oh, love', and neither endearment, nor what Carter had just said,
amounted to very much. He wanted her out—
she must remember that. But this was personal, he'd said. She was confused and didn't
know what to think any more!

'Oh, yes,' he murmured softly, his tone
threatening to melt her bones. 'I had, of course,
had you on my mind before that day.'

'Of course,' she choked.

'But that was the day, that was the time,
when I knew why.'

Desperately she wanted to ask why. But she
was afraid. Carter's look was gentle, his tone
was gentle—but she *had* to remember that his
aim was to get her out!

'You want me out!' she said quickly before
she could allow herself to think of anything
else, and attach any other significance to what
he was saying. 'From the first, you've never

wanted me on the board!' As soon as the words were out, she wanted them back. Carter's gentle look had gone, and changed from surprised to stern.

Then he took what seemed to her to be a steadying kind of breath, and he looked at her. 'I had hoped that—' he began, and broke off. 'I thought if I explained, if I—' He broke off again—and she had the oddest feeling that Carter was feeling a little unsure of his ground. Which just showed her how crazy her thinking had become since she had fallen in love with him, because Carter was always supremely sure about everything. 'Forgive me, Ashlyn. And you're right, of course. I suppose I am rather putting the cart before the horse. But I'm so anxious to—' Again he broke off, and again Ashlyn had the feeling that he was not as one hundred per cent certain as he always was. 'So, to start at the very beginning—if you insist,' he commented, with a trace of a smile that charmed the heart of her, 'I was very much anti Miss Ashlyn Ainsworth before I met you.'

'I love it when you speak the truth!'

'It must be the truth only between you and me, Ashlyn, agreed?'

'Agreed,' she accepted. This time she knew that she would not lie to him again. He caught hold of one of her hands and gave it a light squeeze, and her heart turned over. Carter seemed to forget that he still had her hand in his, for he held it when looking into her eyes, and he continued,

'Hamilton Holdings were desperate that no other company should purchase your father's company. The site it stood on was crucial to our future expansion plans. And, though I objected strongly to having some lightweight female on the board—forgive me, but I'd discovered you hadn't a scrap of business background or training—it was a part of the deal that I was forced to accept to get what I wanted.'

'You accepted, intending to get me out?'

'I accepted taking you with the land—for however long you'd last.'

'You thought I'd soon get fed up with sitting there listening to you men drone on about something far above my head?'

'Something like that,' he admitted. 'But then I met you. I came into the boardroom two and a half months ago—and there you were.'

'I didn't think you'd noticed me,' she confessed.

'Not notice you? Good God, have you looked in your mirror lately?' Ashlyn had not meant to smile, but she just didn't seem able to help it. Carter seemed heartened, for he smiled back, a bone-melting smile, and went on, 'Apart from the fact that I knew exactly where you'd be sitting, one glance your way told me something I just hadn't been prepared for.'

'Oh—what was that?' she asked impulsively.

'That you were beautiful—a quite stunning female.'

'If you thought that, it never showed.' Ashlyn thought she had better say something before he saw how his compliment had thrown her all over the place.

'It wasn't meant to. But I was aware of you through the whole of that meeting—that is,' he qualified, 'the whole time you were there.'

'You—er—noticed I left early,' she murmured, and loved it when he laughed.

'Poor love, you were scarlet—and dripping with water.'

That 'Poor love' was another weakener she could well have done without, though she had hardly expected that he'd have forgotten how she'd drenched the boardroom table, and herself. 'You—um—got up and opened the door for me,' she remembered, her voice going husky again.

'How could I leave you to cope alone? You were a distraction in more ways than one, Miss Ainsworth,' he englightened her.

'How?' The question just popped out.

'Well, for a start, I'm just not used to members of the board nodding off while an important meeting is going on.'

'I found I understood much more of the next meeting,' she felt obliged to tell him.

'I'm glad to hear it,' he answered, and actually grinned. He went on before she had time to pull herself back together again after the devastating effect of that grin, 'But then, at that first meeting, there you were, sailing out, damp, pink-cheeked and mortified—but oh, so proud at the same time. Is it any wonder that I—?' He broke off, and Ashlyn looked at him expectantly. 'That I,' he resumed, 'should start to feel the first stirrings of something which at that time I was unable to give name to?'

Her lips parted. He was looking at her gently again. Her heart thundered. 'Did you—er—was it you who sent Ivy looking for me?' she asked, a great discord of confusion tugging her all ways, making it impossible for her to ask the one question which she wanted so badly to ask: what were those stirrings all about?

'I instructed Lorna to send her,' he owned. 'The next time I saw you was in that crowded lift, and the perfume from your glorious red hair took my mind off business. I had to remind myself that you were a woman I would prefer not to see again.'

Ashlyn stared at him, having no trouble at all remembering how in that lift she had stepped back against him and how she had found it unsettling. Was he saying that he had been very much aware of her too?

'A pity I accepted Geoff Rogers' invitation to join you for lunch,' was the shaky best she could find to say. 'You must have thought you'd never get rid of me.' Suddenly she was remembering something else. 'You had the nerve to warn me off Geoff!' she exclaimed.

'For my sins I thought you were going to let fly with your fists!' It had been a near thing, and she had to smile. She just didn't know where she was when Carter caught hold of her other hand and all of a sudden exclaimed, 'Dammit, Ashlyn, tell me you like me a little— at least!'

Her green eyes went huge. If she hadn't known better she'd have said he sounded frustrated beyond belief, and, yes, tense in the extreme too.

'I disliked you very much—at first,' she quickly owned, seeing no harm in telling him that much.

'With every justification,' he agreed. In fact she had never known him to agree with her so much. 'But that "at first" gives me heart,' he added, and that worried her.

'Well...' She tried an offhand shrug. 'You know how these things are.'

'I'm hoping you're going to tell me.'

He still had a hold of her hands; she tried to pull free, but he would not let go. Ashlyn started to get more seriously worried. Yet her brain seemed to have seized up; she couldn't think of any alternative comment to make. For certain, there was no way she was going to tell him how her dislike of him had changed— barely without she herself knowing—to like and then to love.

It was from pure fear that she trotted out, 'Surely that's your prerogative?'

Carter looked a mite taken aback. But, after a moment, he smiled that smile that made her pulses race. Then he promptly sent her world spinning when, looking deep into her eyes, he said softly, 'I'm longing to tell you how much I like you, Ashlyn.' As pink seeped into her skin, he stretched up a hand to gently stroke her pinkened cheek. 'Your emotional colour tells me that you're not totally immune to me, my dear.' Ashlyn swallowed, struck dumb. 'Are you?' he questioned.

She gave a small cough, but her voice was still husky when she mumbled nervously, 'It's still your prerogative.'

'You want more?' he asked, before conceding, 'Who can blame you?' Sending her brain haywire again, he gently, if briefly, placed his lips against hers. 'Shall I tell you how much, in the weeks before the next board meeting, I had you on my mind? Or how, when I'd already asked Joseph to chair that board meeting because I was otherwise committed, I suddenly found I'd made free time to attend?' She wanted to ask, Because of me? But that was too ridiculous. Of course it wasn't because of her. 'And what did I find when I arrived ...?'

'Me, holding hands with Geoff,' she answered at once. She had never forgotten. 'And you looked through me.'

'What was I supposed to do? I'd warned you to leave him alone—and there you were enjoying some joke with him. I was starting to become irrational, and didn't like it.'

'Irrational?'

'Geoff's brilliant at his job, but a womaniser. He flirts as easily as he breathes. If fault there was, it certainly wasn't yours.'

'Now he tells me!' she exclaimed. 'But why, then, warn me to keep away from him?'

'Didn't I say I was growing irrational? It didn't stop there. I was later certain that Geoff had asked you out to lunch.'

'You're clever,' she agreed. 'Actually, I'd already turned down his offer. But was that the reason you more or less insisted that I lunch with you and Osmund Kogstad?'

Carter smiled ruefully. 'That, and the fact that I didn't much care for the arrogant way you'd been going to walk by with your nose in the air.'

'Honestly!' she gasped.

'In case you're not beginning to get the picture—although with your intelligence I'm sure you are,' he asserted, 'you, Ashlyn Ainsworth, were starting to get to me in a big way.'

Her heart seemed to turn over. 'Was that— er—why you phoned when Lorna had her accident? Was that why you asked me to come in and...?'

'The job in itself was valid enough,' Carter assured her in case she might feel she had been doing something worthless. 'Even if it was a surprise to find out that most of the other directors had jumped on the bandwagon and had calls diverted your way too. I'd seen you charm both Bill Trevitt and Fitz Unger on the first day, remember, and Osmund Kogstad was delighted that not only could you chat away in Norwegian if need be, but that you had such natural warmth. Whether any of us knew it or not, there was a niche with your name on just waiting to be successfully filled.'

That made her feel really good, really valued, and she just had to smile. 'Why, thank you,' she said.

'Don't thank me,' Carter answered. 'The job was valid, as I've told you. Though I have to confess—and it's only lately that I've confessed it to myself,' he admitted, 'I was more keen to have you come and work in this building because seeing you only once every four or five weeks was too long a gap to endure.'

Her eyes shot wide. Oh, glory, oh heavens! 'You—um—wanted to see me more—frequently?'

'I did,' he owned. 'Even on that first day, when I came to your office and wondered what in thunder I was playing at by making some remark about your hairstyle, I had an urge to see you whenever I could.'

'Oh?' she queried. She wanted to ask a whole lot more, but with her emotions suddenly in such a jangled mess she was dreadfully afraid she might ask or say the wrong thing.

'Oh, indeed, little Ashlyn,' Carter murmured ruefully. 'So why, when I wanted to see you more frequently, were you never there when I stopped by?'

'You're exaggerating.'

'Am I? Out to lunch with this man, out to lunch with that one. Flowers arriving...'

'You were—' She broke off, flustered.

'Were?' he pressed.

'I—um—was going to say you were—weren't—er—jealous? But of course you weren't,' she added quickly, going very red and wanting to die.

She nearly did when Carter, as nice as you please, replied, 'My darling—jealous? Of course I was jealous! Even if I wasn't admitting it at the time, I was as jealous as hell!'

'No!' she gasped, staring at him in wonder.

'Aw, come here,' Carter groaned, and, reaching for her, he took her into his arms. 'I know I've barely begun to explain anything yet, but if you won't allow me to just sit and hold you for a while, then I'm certain I'll burst a blood vessel.'

'Oh, we can't have that,' Ashlyn murmured. It was as if she was dreaming, and never wanted to awaken; to be in Carter's arms was utter bliss.

'My love,' he breathed, and, turning her, he looked into her eyes. Then, gently, he kissed her. She did not argue. And when that beautiful kiss ended he looked tenderly into her eyes again. 'I'm sorry,' he apologised softly, 'but I really needed that.'

'You're—um—forgiven.'

'You know you're driving me nuts?'

She laughed, but needed to hear more, so much more. 'You were saying?' she questioned. He held her tightly for a moment as a thank-you for the invitation.

'I was saying that I was growing greener and greener about just about every man you came into contact with,' Carter took up.

'But you weren't admitting it at the time.'

'Certainly not! Did I care who you lunched with? Did it bother me that I should bump into you at the lift with your arms full of flowers? Of course it did,' he smiled.

'The flowers were from Henry for lunching with Donald Yates on his behalf.' Ashlyn saw no reason not to tell him and, fair being fair, she added, 'Um—if it's any consolation, I was certain you'd had lunch—er—a long lunch—with some female.' She could barely believe the look of delight that came to Carter's face.

'*You* were jealous!' he exclaimed.

'Since when has jealously been a solely male right?' she asked.

She nearly dropped when, in his delight and obviously hardly realising what he was saying, he breathed, 'Oh, Ashlyn, dear Ashlyn, I do love you so.' They both halted stock-still. Carter seemed shaken; Ashlyn certainly was. Yet she was the first to find her voice, a poor thing though it was.

'Did you just say—what I thought you said?' she asked croakily.

She still could not believe it when he answered, 'That wasn't the way I'd rehearsed it!'

'You rehearsed ...'

'Ever since early Wednesday morning, even before I knew you'd left, I've been rehearsing how it would go. If you said this, I'd say that. And if you said ... then I'd ... But never did I consider for one moment blurting it out like that. See what you do to me, woman?' he growled.

'I'm—er—glad that I do,' she confessed shyly.

'Oh, sweet love, does that mean what I think it means? What my logical and illogical thoughts— Why would Ashlyn do that if...? and, Surely to have...it must mean... Tell me? Am I going completely insane, or *do* you have some small regard for me?'

He looked strained and she couldn't bear it. 'Oh, Carter, I was all churned up about you before I'd ever met you,' she confessed. 'Then I met you and you made me so angry, and I knew I'd never meet anyone again who could get to me so much emotionally.'

'Don't, for God's sake, leave it there,' he begged.

Ashlyn saw that he seriously needed to be told how it was with her, and willingly went on, 'I was disturbed by you from our very first meeting. Then I started work here, and it got so that the weekends—er—when I stood no chance of seeing you—were very dull indeed.'

'You were missing me—as I missed you!' he pounced, seeming very much cheered.

'I wasn't admitting it.'

'Of course you weren't,' he agreed solemnly. And, still in that same tone, he asked, 'When did you know that you loved me?'

'Oh, I knew that when— Oh-h-h!' she exclaimed She hadn't meant . . .

But Carter had heard and, having led her unwarily into telling him what he was most avid to know, he gave a roar of joy and pulled her closer. 'You *do* love me!' he cried exultantly. 'You do! Darling, darling Ashlyn. Oh, wonderful, wonderful darling,' he breathed. For long, silent moments, not saying another word, he just sat and held her close up against his heart. 'Oh, love, oh, love,' he murmured finally as he pulled back so he could see into her eyes. 'I do so love you,' he breathed. 'Let me hear you say how you feel.'

She felt shaky, nervous, near to tears. Carter loved her, he loved her. 'Oh, I love you, oh, I do,' she whispered. And then Carter kissed her.

It was a heavenly kiss, a tender kiss, and it seemed like a seal, a goodbye to past hurts. Carter looked as shaken as she felt when at last they drew back.

'Did anyone ever tell you about your power to drive men crazy?' Carter murmured, kissing her face, his lips doing incredible things to her right ear.

'Not—er—recently,' she answered chokily. Carter loved her and she was still having a hard time taking it in. 'Um—if it's not too much trouble, I wouldn't mind hearing about it,' she whispered, sorely needing to have her feet back down upon the ground. Though with Carter having declared that he loved her she was quite happy floating where she was.

'Remind me to tell you of the times you repeatedly came between me and my concentration,' he suggested. Her hair was dressed loose and he buried his face in its luxuriant red-gold.

Ashlyn clutched onto him, not caring any longer that he might think her clinging. 'When, for instance?' she laughed joyously, her head back as he transferred his lips to the arch of her throat.

'For instance, that day when you'd lunched with that crook, Corbett. You and I ended up having a spat and you slammed out. Knowing I'd upset you, I just couldn't settle.'

Ashlyn had instant recall. Carter had called it a 'spat' but she had been fuming. 'Oh,' she sighed. 'You were upset that I was upset?'

Carter nodded. 'I came to see you later, intending to try and make things better—only to find you weren't upset at all but were laughing on the phone with some Todd bloke. All my intentions to say something pleasant went up in smoke!'

'You were jealous of Todd! I've known him donkey's years. He's more old chum than boyfriend,' Ashlyn assured him swiftly.

'*Now* you tell me!'

'Ah.' Something suddenly occurred to her. 'You deliberately made me go to Joseph Fulford's home so I shouldn't keep my date with Todd?' she accused lovingly.

'Not that it did me much good—you told me the next morning that he'd waited for you.'

'I lied.'

'You . . .' Carter looked at her, laughed with her. 'Oh, I adore you, Ashlyn Ainsworth,' he said.

And Ashlyn basked in this new-found love and, by degrees, started to grow more confident. So much so that, given she had been at such pains to hide her jealousy, she found that she could say, 'Hmm, you had a heavy date that particular night too, as I recall.'

'You're marvellous,' he beamed. 'I lied.'

'You lied too!'

'Why should you have all the fun?' he grinned. But, perhaps in case she was still feeling a little jealous, he added, 'I confess, my lovely, that I haven't had what I'd call a serious date since that Tuesday when I first cast my eyes on you.'

Ashlyn stared at him. 'Oh, how wonderful,' she sighed, then confessed, 'I thought your business appointment in Paris on Tuesday evening was with the female you'd spent most of that lunchtime in conversation with.'

Carter shook his head. 'My lovely darling, at precisely twelve-thirty that day I'd been delivered the body-blow of knowing that I was in love with you.'

'Oh,' she sighed softly.

He lightly kissed her, resuming, 'My thinking was shattered as I introduced you around, while at the same time I was growing more and more jealous as you charmed the socks off every male in the room.'

'Oh, Carter,' she murmured.

'Believe me, I felt I was going completely off my head, and had to deliberately distance myself from you. Then of course I didn't like it that clearly you'd forgotten my existence.'

'I hadn't at all,' Ashlyn defended gently. 'I was having a jealous battle of my own. You seemed to be hanging onto your lunchtime companion's every word.'

'When what I wanted to do was come and sit beside you. You, I might mention, were sitting between two Frenchmen, and each time I looked—which was more frequently than I

could help—you seemed to be thoroughly enjoying yourself—' He broke off, a dark look
coming to him. 'God, when I think of Boirel
so much as laying a finger on you—'

'I love you,' Ashlyn cut in urgently.

'Oh, my love,' Carter groaned, and held her
safe to him. 'I'd never have taken you to Paris
had I dreamed you would come to such harm.'

'Why did you—take me to Paris, I mean?'
He hadn't needed her knowledge of the French
language, she knew.

'Promise you're not going to hate me?'

'As if I could.'

'I'm certain there were many times you came
close,' he suggested.

'I'm never going to lie to you again,' she
answered, and he smiled, and went on to
answer her question.

'I hadn't, at that time, fully acknowledged
what my feelings for you were,' he confessed.
'I knew, of course, that you were a splendid
hostess. Henry Whitmore has never stopped
singing your praises since you helped him entertain a couple of people to lunch.'

'That's very kind of him.'

'Not kind—fact!' Carter stated. 'As I myself
discovered more fully a week ago when you
hostessed for me at my place. Not that I'd in-

tended asking you to do that when I came looking for you,' he admitted.

'You didn't intend to...?' she gasped.

Carter kissed her cheek, and, liking the feel of her skin, seemed compelled to kiss the other one, before he pulled back to explain, 'I'd been to your office earlier—for nothing specific other than I just felt a need to see you—only you weren't there. So I called back, and it seemed to me then that everyone else was enjoying your company bar me.'

'And *that's* why you invited me to hostess for you?'

'From the reports I was getting, not to mention my own observations when I'd lunched in your company, I knew you'd make an excellent job of it. What I didn't reckon with was how my heart would start to pound when I opened my front door and there you were— the most beautiful woman I had ever seen.'

'Oh, Carter!' she whispered.

They kissed; it seemed the most natural thing to do. They kissed again, and held onto each other, and when that kiss broke Carter held her firmly to him, murmuring endearments in her hair, and telling her of his love for her.

'You're so sweet, shy, sharp, angry—I love all your moods,' he breathed, moving a stray strand of hair gently back from her face.

'I don't think I particularly had moods before I met you,' she laughed.

'Forgive me, villain that I am.' He took all the blame upon himself. 'Though, if it's any consolation, you've had me doing too many times things that I would have believed alien to me.'

'Give me an instance,' she laughed in delight.

'Did I once say you were a minx?' But he went on, 'I was as astonished as you must have been, at the end of that dinner a week ago, to hear myself offering you one of the spare rooms for the night.'

'Oh, I knew you didn't mean anything—er—naughty by it.'

Carter grinned at the adjective she chose, but agreed, 'I didn't. I realised later, though, that it was just that I wanted—needed—to spend more time near you, alone with you.'

'Oh,' she sighed.

'Which then made it a nonsense that, after having been unable to rest when you'd gone until you rang to tell me you were home safe, the following Monday, I found I was resisting the urge to duck in to see you when I was passing on my way in. I had to give in and come and see you in the end, of course.'

Ashlyn had never forgotten. 'I was on the phone to Vezio.'

'And I was as mad as blazes. You were actually daring to think in terms of flying to Italy to be with him that night.'

'I wouldn't have g—' She broke off, a startling thought hitting her. 'That wasn't why... Did you really need a board member with you? No, I don't bel—'

'Neither did I.' Carter, to her amazement, was right on her wavelength. 'To start with I'm sure I only rang you on the intercom to check that, after our fight—and knowing I'd be in France for three or four days—you were all right. But the next thing I knew, even as we were talking, was that I was suddenly starting to think, to hell with you going to Italy that night, albeit I couldn't at that moment come up with any business reason; and I decided you'd fly to Paris with me instead.'

'It was a lovely flight,' she remembered dreamily.

'But you took exception to our sharing the same apartment.'

'It wasn't that exactly,' she quickly owned. 'It was more that being together, living so close together, I was afraid you might get a hint of how I truly felt about you.'

'You knew you were in love with me then?' Carter picked up with the quickness she had always associated with him.

'Ooops,' she smiled, but since he knew now how she felt about him anyway she continued, 'It was all so new to me. It was only that day, when I put the phone down after you'd told me you'd see me at the airport, that—it was there. I just knew that I was in love with you.'

'My sweet darling,' Carter breathed, kissing her hair, kissing her face.

'You kissed my cheek then—in that apartment—when we arrived.'

'I couldn't help it. There you were, gorgeous, innocent, uncaring of money. I just had to,' he said simply. 'But almost immediately realised I'd better check such impulses.'

'But when we came back from dining with Solène and Luc you kissed me again,' she reminded him, adding, with all honesty, 'Well, I helped a bit, by kissing your cheek, I suppose.'

'And what was meant as only a light kiss after that got a little out of hand,' he admitted. 'I barely slept all night for thinking about you.'

'Was that why you were such a grouch the next morning?'

'How else would I be, sweet love? You'd got me so I didn't know where I was. I just couldn't have you wrecking my concentration at what was a very important meeting.'

'So you told me to go and shop!'

'And felt a swine for doing it—so I just had to tell you I needed you there at lunch. And— my darling, the moment I saw you I knew then that I was heart and soul in love with you.'

'Oh, Carter,' she sighed blissfully.

She knew more bliss when he revealed, 'Knowing you'd be too much of a distraction if I took you with me to my business meeting that night, I came to see you on my way out. And there you were, in complete contrast to the sophisticated woman I'd seen at lunchtime, all scrubbed and cuddly—and I fell in love with you all over again.'

'Truly?' she gasped.

'Oh, love,' he cried, and kissed her, oh, so tenderly. And kissed her again. Many minutes later, he seemed to remember there were still some matters to be cleared up. 'Where was I?' he asked.

Ashlyn sighed, her cheeks pleasantly flushed. 'I—er—you were telling me how you fell in love with me all over again,' she reminded him softly.

'Sweetheart.' He kissed her, and when she immediately began to respond again he breathed, 'My God, Ashlyn, you do a man's brain in.' And he seemed to love it when she laughed lightly with delight. 'But, to go back, it was then that I realised I'd better get my business done with all speed so as to get back to England sooner. Then I hoped to see if there was any remote possibility that you might care for me.'

'You—um—hadn't guessed that I—er—cared quite a lot for you?'

'Not then,' Carter answered. 'You'd sent me away with your acid "Have a good time—with your business!" ringing in my ears. It was total distraction,' he said ruefully. 'There was I, trying to concentrate, and there were these three words "with your business" going around in my head. Did you not believe I was attending a business appointment? Did you think I'd gone to meet some female? Were you jealous? Did you care? I finished my business as soon as I could and rushed back to the apartment, knowing that I was going to have to take things very slowly. Perhaps we'd dine after all. Perhaps I'd show you something of Paris by night.'

'Only I wasn't in. Oh, Carter, I wish I had been.'

'So do I, my dear love. Instead, while I was going quietly demented, you were fighting off that lecher Boirel!'

'And I got back to the apartment, only to have a fight with you.'

'Only for a few minutes, until I'd got myself under control after the relief of seeing you. Poor, poor love. Then, while I was doing what I could to comfort you, my heart started to race with hope when you said you wanted to be close to me. Was it just that you were in need of decent human warmth, or did you care a little for me?'

'Which did you decide?' Ashlyn asked huskily.

'I didn't. Couldn't. You were at your most vulnerable just then. I knew I had to look after you. I wanted to look after you. But I kissed you a little so that you'd know that not all men were lusting monsters—I think I had some vague notion at the start that I'd hold you until you were asleep, and then go.'

'It—didn't work out like that,' Ashlyn offered shyly.

'It did not,' Carter agreed. 'Before I knew it we were in the throes of lovemaking. But, even

though my conscience had been getting at me
for some while, it wasn't until I heard you actually *apologising* for your wonderful inno-
cence that I was shaken into wondering, What
in God's name am I doing? It was then that I
realised I hadn't been thinking at all—but that
for you, for me, for my hope for the future, I
had better start—and quick. It was as my brain
started to reactivate itself and I tried to end our
lovemaking that I knew you needed a sedative,
not a stimulant. You'd been traumatised and
had been shaking after what you'd been
through. And now, possibly still in shock, you
were trembling from an emotion that was new
to you, and which was probably confusing you
more than a little.'

'I don't remember feeling confused,' she
owned gently.

'Well, I was,' Carter confessed. 'All I knew
for certain was that because in effect you
worked for me, because it was I who'd brought
you to France, but, most of all, because you
were most dear, most precious to me, I should
be protecting you. Almost too late, my lovely
Ashlyn, I realised I was taking advantage of
your shock, your vulnerability, and was not
protecting you at all. Later, you might have

hated me——and it was not your hate that I wanted.'

'I could never hate you——not now,' Ashlyn murmured. 'Though all I knew then——because I'd been so clinging——was that I would never be able to look you in the face again.'

'Oh, my proud love! Is that why you left and refused to see me?'

'I wouldn't have done if I'd known,' she answered openly——and was soundly kissed for her trouble.

'Instead you returned to England, leaving me tearing my hair out because you'd put up a barrier which I didn't know how to get through.'

'You managed it, though,' she smiled. But added quickly, 'There isn't any board meeting this morning, is there?'

'No, my love,' he smiled. Then he paused, and he was never more serious than when he went on, 'And neither you nor I will be here for the next one.'

'You do know that the first I heard that I was to be a board member was when my father——' She broke off, blinked. 'Why won't we be here for the next board meeting?' she asked, totally innocently.

'Because, my darling, we'll be away on our honeymoon,' Carter replied.

'Honeymoon?' she gasped.

'You do agree to marry me?' Carter asked, his voice quick suddenly, strained and urgent.

She smiled, and sighed with pure joy. 'I'm sure the board can manage without us for a week or two,' she accepted.

'More than a month or two,' Carter growled.

'Oh, yes to that too,' Ashlyn said softly.

'Kiss me,' he demanded.

He was her chairman, her love—his wish was her command.

MILLS & BOON® PUBLISH EIGHT
LARGE PRINT TITLES A MONTH.
THESE ARE THE EIGHT TITLES
FOR AUGUST 1997

MISTAKEN FOR A MISTRESS
Jacqueline Baird

LOVERS' LIES
Daphne Clair

RUNAWAY HONEYMOON
Ruth Jean Dale

NIGHT OF SHAME
Miranda Lee

THE DAUGHTER OF THE MANOR
Betty Neels

LOOKING AFTER DAD
Elizabeth Oldfield

A BUSINESS ENGAGEMENT
Jessica Steele

THE GUILTY WIFE
Sally Wentworth

MILLS & BOON® PUBLISH EIGHT
LARGE PRINT TITLES A MONTH.
THESE ARE THE EIGHT TITLES
FOR SEPTEMBER 1997

CRAVING JAMIE
Emma Darcy

THE SECOND BRIDE
Catherine George

HIS BROTHER'S CHILD
Lucy Gordon

THE SECRET WIFE
Lynne Graham

WEDDING DAZE
Diana Hamilton

KISS AND TELL
Sharon Kendrick

FINN'S TWINS!
Anne McAllister

AN INNOCENT CHARADE
Patricia Wilson